*Wishbone could hear the loud,
roaring sound of the bulldozer
as it churned up the earth.*

He spotted David Barnes by the large tree, video camera in hand. "Are you getting it all on tape?" Wishbone asked. David didn't answer, concentrating instead on videotaping the destruction of the area around the tree.

What a mess! Wishbone thought. *I hope we're not too late.*

Wishbone could see how much damage had already been done as he leaped over fallen branches. Felled trees and uprooted bushes and shrubs were scattered around. Piles of dirt towered over him.

"Hey! You with the bulldozer!" Wishbone shouted. "Nobody digs here but me."

Wishbone eyed the bulldozer and couldn't help noticing that the two of them were not evenly matched.

"I am one dog against all odds!" Wishbone said as he leaped into the bulldozer's jaws. . . .

The Adventures of WISHBONE™

HOMER SWEET HOMER

by Carla Jablonski
Based on the teleplay by Stephanie Simpson
Inspired by *The Odyssey*
by Homer

WISHBONE™ created by Rick Duffield

Big Red Chair Books™, *A Division of Lyrick Publishing*™

This book is a work of fiction. The characters, incidents, and dialogues are products of the author's imagination and are not to be construed as real. Any resemblance to actual events or persons, living or dead, is entirely coincidental.

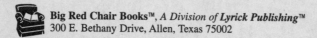 **Big Red Chair Books**™, *A Division of Lyrick Publishing*™
300 E. Bethany Drive, Allen, Texas 75002

Edited by Pam Pollack

Copy edited by Jonathon Brodman

Cover design by Lyle Miller

Interior illustrations by Don Punchatz

Wishbone photograph by Carol Kaelson

Library of Congress Catalog Card Number: 97-81253

ISBN: 1-57064-392-X

First printing: July 1998

10 9 8 7 6 5 4 3 2

Printed in the United States of America

For Matthew
and Michelle

FROM THE BIG RED CHAIR . . .

Oh . . . hi! Wishbone here. You caught me right in the middle of some of my favorite things—books. Let me welcome you to THE ADVENTURES OF WISHBONE. In each of these books, I have adventures with my friends in Oakdale and imagine myself as a character in one of the greatest stories of all time. This story takes place in the spring, when Joe is twelve and he and his friends are in the sixth grade—during the first season of my television show.

In *HOMER SWEET HOMER*, I imagine I'm Odysseus, the warrior-hero from Homer's epic poem *THE ODYSSEY*. As Odysseus, my goal is to sail home to Greece after ten long years of fighting in the far-off Trojan War. But first I must face a one-eyed monster; an angry sea god; a six-headed serpent; and much more. Hold on to your life jacket as we sail homeward!

You're in for a real treat, so pull up a chair and a snack and sink your teeth into *HOMER SWEET HOMER!*

CHAPTER ONE

"Ow! Emily! Slow down!" Wishbone's head hit the top of the pet carrier as Emily Barnes raced along the bumpy street. Wishbone sat caged in the middle of the red wagon Emily pulled behind her. As usual, the five-year-old girl ignored him.

Emily was David Barnes's younger sister. David was a next-door neighbor and good friend of Wishbone and Joe Talbot. The Jack Russell terrier lived with Joe and Joe's mom, Ellen. Wishbone considered Joe his best friend, and he knew Joe felt the same way toward him.

Emily is never going to listen to me, Wishbone thought. He knew from past experience that Emily could be very stubborn. She liked to do things her own way. *Once she gets an idea,* Wishbone observed, *she doesn't give it up easily. She hangs on to it as if it were a prize bone.*

Suddenly Wishbone's head whipped around. "Hey! What's going on?" *That is my street,* he thought.

So why is Emily passing it by? "Uh, Emily, I don't want to be a backseat driver, but you were supposed to take the turn back there. This isn't the way home."

Emily charged forward. Wishbone's heart began to beat faster. His fur bristled as he realized that she was not going to head for home.

Where is she taking me? the white-with-brown-and-black-spots terrier wondered. *And why?* With Emily, a dog had to be prepared for anything—and everything. Wishbone pushed his nose through the bars of the pet carrier. "This is a test of my emergency broadcast system. Help!"

"You're my dog now, Wishbone," Emily said. She took another quick turn around a corner. Her short, thick braids swung from one side to the other as she dashed down the sidewalk.

Wishbone's ears flicked forward and he sat straight up. *Did she just say what I think she just said? I'm*

her *dog now? Okay, I've been patient, but enough is enough. It's time for more drastic action.*

He barked as loudly as he could. "Help! Anybody! Help! Dognapping in progress!"

No one seemed to hear him.

I've got to get out of here. Wishbone gripped the bars in his teeth, rattling them hard, trying to attract attention.

"And you know what else, Wishbone?" Emily declared. "We're *never* going home!"

"What?" The situation was even worse than he thought. "What do you mean, we're never going home? I like home. So do you. Home is good."

Still, Emily kept going.

I'm in real trouble, Wishbone thought. He barked out one side of the cage and then the other. But the streets were empty. There was no one nearby to hear his cries or rescue him. *I'm on my own,* he realized. *I'll just have to rescue myself.*

Emily picked up speed, moving so quickly that Wishbone slid inside the pet carrier. "Whoa!" Wishbone struggled to stay on all fours.

Then he saw that they were heading into the wooded area leading to Jackson Park. Emily followed the narrow paths through the bushes. Branches scraped against the dog's cage.

Wishbone barked loudly. "Dognapping is a very serious crime! Not to mention really, really bad behavior. Wow! Are *you* going to get into trouble!"

Emily paid no attention. The wagon almost flew over the rough ground, bouncing over roots and fallen branches. Wishbone tried his best to keep himself from falling over.

"Hey! I'm getting seasick back here—I mean wagon-sick. Slow down, or I'll have to add speeding to my list of charges against you!"

Finally, Emily came to a stop in a large clearing. Wishbone recognized the place. A beautiful old tree spread its graceful, sheltering branches over the area. A tire swing dangled from its lowest branch. Wishbone and his friends spent a lot of time there. It was a special place for all of them, especially for Joe. It was Joe's dad who had hung that tire swing. He had set it up a few years earlier, shortly before he died. Now that he was gone, Joe often came there to try to remember the happy times they had spent together.

Emily turned to face Wishbone. Her big brown eyes gazed at him through the bars of the cage. "We're going to live here, Wishbone," she told him. "Right under this tree. Forever."

"I *have* a home already, thank you very much." He scratched furiously at the bottom of the cage. "There's got to be a way to get out of here." He stretched a paw through the bars of the cage. "Can I reach the latch? No. And even if I could . . . no thumbs."

He nosed along the bottom bars, searching for any crack or break in the imprisoning cage. Nothing.

"I'm going to have to come up with a very clever plan to get out of this one." He peered longingly out of the cage, past Emily, at the big old tree, at freedom.

Wishbone lay down to think of a plan. Something about this whole situation seemed familiar.

"Hmm . . . an adventurer determined to get home, facing many problems along the way. This whole thing reminds me of the difficult journey of the ancient Greek hero-warrior, Odysseus."

Odysseus is the hero of the epic poem *The Odyssey,* written by the ancient Greek poet Homer. The word *odyssey* means a long journey. And Odysseus had quite a long journey. It took him ten years to get home to Greece after fighting in the Trojan War! Wow! Talk about being late for dinner!

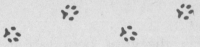

Held prisoner in the pet carrier, it was easy for Wishbone to imagine he really was Odysseus. He promised to find a way home, just as Odysseus did.

As Emily dragged the wagon around the tree, Wishbone shut his eyes and imagined he was some-where else. The rocking motion of the pet carrier became the rolling of the ancient waves. The cool breeze that ruffled his fur was the ocean wind.

Yes, he thought, just as Odysseus thought, *the troubles I am facing are great ones, but I will get home—no matter what!*

CHAPTER TWO

Odysseus, the great hero-warrior and king of Ithaca, stood at the railing of his ship, surveying the horizon. He planted his four feet firmly on the deck to roll with the waves. A light breeze ruffled his fur. His whiskers tingled with the stinging dampness of the salt spray.

He had led his men to victory in the great battle at Troy, far from his homeland of Ithaca, a Greek island. Ten long years they fought. Now, as captain of this ship, he would lead his forces on the dangerous journey home.

He placed his front paws on the railing and looked over the side. He saw the oars poking out of their small holes in the side of the wooden hull. He watched their steady rise and fall in the deep blue water. He felt sadness as he realized how many oarsmen were missing. Where once more than one hundred had powered the mighty ship, the crew had shrunk to only fifty.

Odysseus shook his head. *We lost so many brave warriors during the battle,* he thought. *I am determined that we shall lose no more.*

Odysseus barked to get the midship sailor's attention. He raised a paw, gesturing for the huge sail to be unfurled. Instantly, the sailors on deck leaped into action. They loosened the thick ropes, and the heavy linen sail dropped into place. Odysseus felt the ship move forward with a burst of speed.

May as well use all the power we can, Odysseus figured. *After all, it's not as if we're going to get a speeding ticket out here.*

Odysseus aimed his nose directly into the breeze, trying to catch a scent. "I don't like these winds," he said. *Could our great victory in the Trojan War have upset one of the gods?* he wondered. But which one? And why? There were many gods, each with supernatural powers. He knew the gods, just like ordinary people, had their arguments and their favorites. He had been supported and defended by the goddess of wisdom, Athena. She took his side in arguments with the gods. Sometimes she helped him in battle and at sea. *But this voyage has already taken longer than it should have,* he thought. *Perhaps an angry god is putting extra challenges in our path.*

"But I shall meet every one of them," Odysseus said into the winds.

Nothing would keep him from returning home to his kingdom in Ithaca; to his beloved wife, Queen Penelope; and to his son, Telemachus. Nothing. No sea creatures, no interfering gods, no unknown enemy, no winds, rains, or tidal waves. He was *that* determined.

Now Odysseus and his men were heading into the harbor of a small, densely wooded island. The war hero had noticed smoke rising above the treetops. "Where there's smoke, there's fire," he said, pointing a paw at the island.

"And where there's fire, there must be people," an oarsman added.

"And if there are people," another crewman said, "there will be food."

Odysseus nodded. The delays in their journey had seriously cut back on their supplies. He hoped this island community would be generous in sharing whatever it could give.

Odysseus climbed the pole from which the sail was hung. With his sharp eyesight, Odysseus noticed the mouth of a cave gaping in the very large boulders near the water's edge. In front of the cave was a large area filled with goats, cattle, and sheep. *This must be the home of one of the shepherds,* Odysseus thought.

He shouted an order. "Enter the harbor here!"

Odysseus gazed at the very large, rough stones that formed a natural pen for the animals. *It took great strength to place the huge rocks among the mighty trees! The people of this island must be very strong, indeed.* Odysseus climbed back down. He decided to bring a small leather-sack container of magical wine on shore with him—just in case he needed a special potion to help him. A grateful friend whose family Odysseus had once rescued had given him the wine as a gift.

The men dragged a small boat ashore, then approached the cave.

"Hello!" Odysseus called. "Anybody home?"

No one answered.

"Maybe our host is somewhere near the back of the cave and can't hear us," Odysseus suggested. "After all, the place seems huge. Let's go in and call out to him again."

Odysseus led his companions into the cave. A large section served as a pen for sheep, cattle, and goats. Big baskets woven from vines and thin tree branches hung from the rough rock walls. Odysseus's nose twitched at the many smells hanging in the air.

"Look at all this cheese!" an oarsman cried.

"And pail after pail of milk!" another called.

"And all the cattle just ready for roasting," a third added. "There's more than enough food here to last us for our long journey home."

Before Odysseus could reply, a gigantic shadow filled the mouth of the cave. The huge figure suddenly hurled a load of heavy tree trunks into the center of the cave. Odysseus's fur stood on end. *Maybe stopping in here wasn't one of my better ideas!* He and his men scurried into hiding, pressing themselves against the cold rock walls of the cave.

Boom! Boom! Boom! The ground quaked and shook violently as the master of the cave entered. He stepped aside to allow his flock of animals to dash in. "Inside— now, you lazy animals!" he roared. "Don't make me come and get you!"

Odysseus's ears flattened at the horrible sound of the voice. The creature's yowl seemed to shake the entire world! Heart pounding, Odysseus watched as the giant moved an enormous slab of rock in front of the cave entrance.

We're trapped! Odysseus realized with growing horror. *A team of twenty horses would not have the strength to move that boulder. My twelve men who came ashore and I could never even make it budge.*

Then the giant turned. And, for the first time, Odysseus got a good look at his face. The sight made the warrior-hero want to howl with fear. With great effort, however, he managed to stay silent.

The giant towering above them was a cyclops—a one-eyed monster who was part of a rough, untamed, and dangerous breed that respected no one's laws, not even those of the gods. The creature's huge eye bulged in the middle of its broad forehead. Odysseus now realized what island they were on—the island of the feared cyclops!

The cyclops bent over and started to build a fire. The flickering shadows threw light on Odysseus and his crew. They huddled in terror against the cave walls.

"Who are you?" thundered the cyclops.

Odysseus felt his fur bristle, his body preparing for whatever danger might come next. "Our ship has been blown off course on our way home," Odysseus explained. "We have come here for help, and for the kindness the god Zeus himself would expect any host to offer strangers."

"Ha! Ha! Ha!" The force of the cyclops's rough laughter nearly knocked Odysseus over. "What do I care for Zeus, the king of all gods, or anyone else, for that matter? I make my own rules."

I'd better forget the guest-gift idea, Odysseus told himself.

The cyclops leaned over to get a better look at Odysseus. The single eye stared down at him. Odysseus stared back. He didn't even blink.

"Where is your ship?" the cyclops demanded.

"It crashed on the rocks," Odysseus lied. *Right. Like I'm really going to tell a raging one-eyed monster the location of our only way of escape.*

"Humph." The giant stood upright again. In one swift move, he snatched up two of the crewmen. He reared back his arm and then smashed them to the ground. Then he scooped up the men's shattered bodies, and as Odysseus watched helplessly, the giant swallowed them.

Odysseus gripped his sword in his teeth, but then he remained still. He knew armed combat would be useless against a creature whose strength was greater than his own.

The unlucky warriors must have made a satisfying

meal, Odysseus thought grimly as he watched the cyclops lie down and quickly fall asleep.

"Let's do away with him now," an oarsman whispered. "Now, while he sleeps."

Odysseus shook his head and pointed at the enormous boulder blocking the entrance to the cave. "We would be trapped in here forever," he said. "No, this is the time for cleverness, not brute force."

Odysseus glanced around the cave. His eyes settled on a tree trunk that was near the fire. It gave him an idea.

Odysseus trotted over to the tree trunk and sank his teeth into the bark. *Trees,* Odysseus thought. *Always there when you need them.* His men jumped to his aid to drag the large piece of timber closer to the fire.

"Sharpen it to a deadly point. Then hold it deep within the fire," Odysseus instructed. "The wood is green and will not burn in the flames. Keep it there until it glows with red-hot heat."

The cyclops stirred, and Odysseus whipped his head around to gaze at the enemy. The giant was waking up!

The cyclops yawned. He rubbed his one huge eye and smacked his enormous lips. Then he raised himself up and reached out and grabbed a crewman. Once again, all Odysseus could do was watch in horror. The unfortunate man screamed and screamed as the cyclops squeezed the life out of him with his huge, powerful fist. Then the cyclops popped the limp figure into his gaping mouth.

The cyclops looked around the cave until his one frightening eye fell on Odysseus. "Now that I have had my snack, it's time for you to tell me who you are," he boomed.

Odysseus bit down his anger. He had to stay absolutely calm—or his plan would never work. "Share a drink with me, and I will share my secrets with you." *Well, maybe not all of them,* he added silently.

Odysseus knew the cyclops wouldn't be able to resist the invitation. Odysseus held up the leather sack that contained the magic wine.

The cyclops greedily snatched up the sack and gulped down the wine.

This guy needs to learn some manners, Odysseus thought. *He could sure use some obedience school training. But at least part of the plan is working. The wine will put the monster back to sleep long enough for us to take action.*

Odysseus watched the cyclops lean against the cave wall and slide down. "Going down?" Odysseus muttered. "Next stop, ground floor." The cyclops finally landed flat with a loud thud.

"So you enjoyed the drink I offered?" Odysseus asked. He could hear his men creeping around the cave, getting into place, waiting for the magical wine to have its full effect.

"I enjoyed it very much, indeed," the cyclops responded. "But now you must tell me your name. If you will tell me your name, I will give you your rightful guest gift."

Fat chance, Odysseus thought. He knew not to trust this monster. "Cyclops, since you have promised me my gift, I shall tell you what my famous name is. It is Noman! That is, I answer to no man."

The cyclops let out an enormous yawn, and

Odysseus's tail wagged in anticipation. The magical wine was casting its spell.

The cyclops slumped farther down, until he was lying flat on the ground. "I promised you your gift, and here it is," he mumbled sleepily. "I will eat Noman after I eat all his friends."

"You will eat no man at all," Odysseus said under his breath.

The cyclops belched loudly. His huge eye blinked once, twice, three times, then stayed shut. In just a few moments, under the full effect of the magic wine, the cyclops slept soundly.

Odysseus called out the signal. "Now!"

The men lifted the sharpened tree trunk out of the fire and raised it up onto their shoulders. Taking care to avoid making contact with the smoldering tip, Odysseus guided his crew's aim. Then they rushed toward the sleeping giant. They stabbed the glowing-hot point of the huge, deadly trunk directly into the monster's single, grotesque eye.

"*Aaaaaaaagghh!*" The cyclops shrieked in pain, his tortured cry causing the entire cave to rumble. He grabbed the tree trunk, trying desperately to yank it out of his eye. But the men clung tightly to their weapon. Using all their weight, they forced the wood deeper into the oozing wound.

Then, with an enormous roar, the cyclops pushed himself up. Odysseus and his men dropped away from the smoldering tree trunk and dashed out of the path of the angry monster. Still shrieking in pain, the giant tore the tree trunk from his eye and hurled it to the ground as if it were but a mere stick.

21

"Yes!" Just as Odysseus had hoped, the cyclops stumbled over to the entrance of the cave.

"Help me!" the cyclops screamed. "Please! Someone! I'm under attack!" He grabbed the boulder and threw it aside.

Freedom. There it was, just a few yards away.

Odysseus could hear the thundering roar of massive footsteps approaching the cave. More giants were on their way to help the cyclops!

"Who is attacking you?" a voice called out to the cyclops. "Who is your enemy?"

Odysseus held his breath, waiting for the answer. This was make-or-break time.

"Noman!" the cyclops replied. "Noman is here. Noman is attacking me!"

The giants muttered among themselves, and Odysseus could hear a few giant-sized gasps.

"Polyphemus," one of them called, for that was the cyclops's name, "if you are alone and no man is there, surely your troubles have been sent by some angry god."

"We cannot help you and bring down that curse upon ourselves!" another shouted.

As the giants lumbered off, Odysseus was filled with relief and pride that his clever trick had worked. *That was a brilliant bit of strategy,* Odysseus thought. *I fooled them all.*

Odysseus's tail stopped in mid-wag when he realized what the cyclops was doing. The giant planted himself solidly at the cave entrance. As the goats and sheep hurried by him on their way out, he ran his huge hands over each one.

"You will not sneak by me!" the cyclops thundered at Odysseus. "I'll have you yet!"

But Odysseus was already plotting an escape. He would not allow his crew to be trapped. He quickly instructed each of his men to find the largest sheep they could. "The furrier, the better. We will sneak out clinging to the bellies of the animals."

Odysseus watched an oarsman catch a large sheep. The creature let out a low bleat, but stood still as the young man crawled under it. Grabbing a strong vine, Odysseus tied the man into position under the sheep's stomach. Once the man was fastened securely, other crew members fluffed up the sheep's thick fur, covering the man completely.

"Hey, you look good in white fur," Odysseus told the hidden man.

Odysseus gave the sheep a quick pat, sending it toward the mouth of the cave—and the cyclops. He held his breath, waiting to see if his plan would work.

Polyphemus felt the sheep as it passed. "Okay," the blinded monster grumbled. "You're one of my flock, not one of those horrible friends of Noman."

Yes! Odysseus cheered silently. *Sheep make excellent crew-carriers!* He quickly helped tie the other men into place, then sent the sheep on their way out of the cave. He waited until he was sure each of his remaining crewmen had escaped. Then he grabbed a large sheep. Gripping the frightened animal's belly, Odysseus slid underneath it. Slowly, a little off balance with the added weight, the sheep stumbled toward the cave entrance and the still-moaning cyclops. As the sheep passed by the giant, he patted the animal all over, as he had done to the others before it. Odysseus tried not to twitch a whisker, and he willed his tail to stay still.

"If only you could speak," the cyclops raged at the sheep. "You could tell me where that rascal Noman is in my cave. I'd smash him to bits!"

Odysseus was sure the cyclops meant every word. The warrior-hero was glad that the sheep did *not* speak. But he hoped the cyclops would hurry and release the animal. He wasn't sure how much longer he could keep his grip.

"You hear me, Noman?" The cyclops stepped into the center of the now empty cave. The sheep immediately dashed out the cave entrance. "You are still my prisoner!"

Wanna bet? Odysseus thought. The moment he and the sheep were outside the cave, Odysseus let go of the animal's fur. *This is one weird form of transportation,* he thought, as he scrambled to his four feet. *I don't think it's going to catch on.*

Odysseus raced to the ship and leaped aboard, his eyes bright with triumph. Before ordering the men to get under way, he glanced back to the cyclops's cave. At the sight of the savage creature, Odysseus couldn't resist insulting the cyclops. "Polyphemus! If anyone asks you who has defeated you, it was not Noman. It was I—the brave Odysseus!"

With a howl of fury, the cyclops ripped off a hunk of the island's cliff and hurled it at the ship. Then the boulder landed just a few feet from the bow. The action sent up a towering wave that crashed onto Odysseus and the crew.

The men screamed and clutched their oars,

stroking hard, trying not to capsize. "Have no fear, men!" Odysseus shouted. "He cannot reach us now."

But the cyclops called back with a terrible threat: "I shall tell my father, Poseidon, god of the sea, about the terrible treatment that I received at your hands, Odysseus!"

These remarks worried Odysseus. Poseidon was a powerful god. Being on his bad side during a long sea voyage could be a problem. *Have I gone too far this time?* Odysseus wondered. *Maybe I should not have told the cyclops my name.*

But still, he thought, it was only right to take credit where credit was due. He gave his body a sharp shake, spraying worry and water from his fur. He could not let his men see that the cyclops's threat had worried him.

"My brave companions!" Odysseus declared. "We have faced many dangers before and have proven that even enemies with greater strength cannot defeat us. I promise that we shall see home again!"

The men cheered. Odysseus took his usual place at the helm. As he gazed across the choppy waves, he wondered how many more obstacles they would have to overcome before he could keep his promise.

CHAPTER THREE

Wishbone poked his nose through the bars of the cage that held him prisoner. "Okay, Emily, I'm willing to negotiate."

Emily gazed back at him.

"So, Emily . . ." Wishbone cocked an ear. "What'll it be? How about if . . . I let you play with my squeaky book? My prize collection of chew bones?" He studied the little girl, hoping for some sign of agreement. Clearly she wasn't going for it. He'd have to come up with a more attractive offer. "Okay, Emily, this is my final idea. Will you let me out of this cage if—"

Before Wishbone offered to cough up his best squeaky toy, a rustling in the nearby bushes caught his attention. His ears pricked up.

"Wishbone!"

Yes! Familiar voices! Humans are on their way to the rescue!

"Wishbone! Where are you, boy?"

"Joe! Over here!" Wishbone barked furiously. "This little bandit is holding me captive."

Wishbone watched in great relief as Joe Talbot, David Barnes, and Samantha Kepler came out from the thick bushes. *Those three will have no trouble handling this situation,* Wishbone thought.

Samantha, Sam for short, wore jeans and a blue flannel shirt over a white T-shirt. She had her long blond hair tied in a ponytail and tucked under a baseball cap. David's dark skin and almond-shaped brown eyes were just like his younger sister's—only he was a lot taller. Wishbone's best friend, Joe, had on his favorite jeans and gray hooded sweatshirt.

Wishbone's tail began to wag as his three friends headed straight toward him.

"Uh-oh." Emily moved away from the wagon.

"Emily, what are you doing?" David demanded.

Wishbone circled around inside the cage. "Wait till you hear this one, guys," he said. "You're not going to believe it. Go ahead, Emily, tell them your plan."

"I'm going to live here with Wishbone," Emily declared.

Wishbone gazed up at Joe. "What did I tell you?"

Joe raised an eyebrow and exchanged a look with David. David shook his head.

"Wishbone is not your dog," David explained to Emily.

"Hear that?" Wishbone said.

"He is now," Emily insisted.

Now Wishbone shook *his* head. *She's putting up some fight to keep me,* Wishbone thought. *Well, who can blame her? After all, I am charming, clever, brave. Oh,*

27

yeah—and still stuck inside this awful cage! He began to bark again.

David gave Emily a hard look. "Emily, Wishbone is Joe's dog. He let you *borrow* him for pet day at kindergarten. He did not *give* him to you."

Emily crossed her arms and stood in front of the wagon. "But I *want* him."

"I can't believe my own sister is a dognapper," David said.

Wishbone had to admire the girl's firmness in carrying out her plan, but enough already! "Okay people, let's cut the chitchat and free the dog!" Wishbone pawed at the bottom of the cage, barking and yelping.

Joe bent down and unlatched the cage.

"Finally!" Wishbone dashed out of the cage and leaped from the wagon. "I'm free! Oh, yes! Trees! Grass! Fresh dirt!"

He raced around the giant oak tree. Grass had never felt so good beneath his feet. With a big rush of energy, he leaped through the tire swing.

"Huh? What's that?" A sound in the underbrush caught Wishbone's attention. He was distracted from celebrating his freedom. Several men walked into the clearing. They were led by a man in a gray suit, who was speaking rapidly into a portable phone. Wishbone recognized the man as Mr. King, a local businessman.

"We'll have to bulldoze all of this underbrush to have a path for the heavy equipment," Mr. King said. Then he motioned at the large tree with the phone. "This tree is going to give us some problems. All right, let's get ready for the whole area to be paved."

The men following him nodded, then scattered around the area.

Mr. King walked right through the circle of friends, then turned to address them. "I'm afraid you kids will have to get out of the way."

What does he think he's doing? Wishbone thought. He trotted after Mr. King. "Excuse me. May I ask you to move? Do you have any idea what you're standing on?" Wishbone dug furiously between Mr. King's feet.

"My shoes!" Mr. King exclaimed.

"I know it's here. . . . Yes!" Wishbone retrieved a dirty, chewed-up sock. He trotted proudly over to Joe and laid the prize at his pal's feet. "I want you to have it, really I do. It's a thank-you for getting me out of Emily's clutches. Though," he added, "I did have the situation pretty much under control. . . ."

"Ugh! Wishbone, what *is* that?" Joe asked.

Wishbone looked up and cocked his head to one side. "It's a sock," Wishbone explained patiently. "It's some of my best burying work."

"Here's a suggestion. Why don't you kids take your dog and go home?" Mr. King said.

That doesn't sound like a suggestion to me, Wishbone thought. *It sounds like an order.*

"But isn't this part of Jackson Park?" Joe asked, as he glanced around.

"Nope," Mr. King replied. "It belongs to Suitor Development Corporation. And you'll be happy to know that in just a few days we'll be breaking ground for a brand-new Tastee Oasis."

"Here? Great!" David said.

Hmm . . . Wishbone thought, *I'm usually on the*

side of food—but not if it means saying good-bye to all of these trees.

"But first," Mr. King continued, "we need to do some clearing so we can get the whole site laid out for parking lots and other stores."

Joe saw the construction crew placing the markers around the area. He ran a hand through his thick brown hair in disbelief. "You're going to pave this whole place?"

"Of course," Mr. King responded.

"What?" Sam exclaimed.

Wishbone leaped up and raced to each of his favorite spots. He began to bark as he crisscrossed the area. "This is my burial ground! I've got stuff every-where!" *They can't pave all of this over! Surely they'll listen to reason!*

Emily dashed over to the big tree, flinging herself against it. "This tree is mine! Leave it alone!"

"Trust me," Wishbone warned Mr. King. "You don't want to mess with her."

Mr. King ignored the terrier. "Sorry, sweetheart," Mr. King told Emily. "But in a few days this tree will be history."

"It already *is* history," Sam said. "It's nearly two hundred years old."

"Wow! That's nearly fourteen hundred in dog years." Wishbone placed a paw on the tree, feeling its rough bark. "You look good for your age. You don't look a day over a thousand."

"My mom says that this tree is one of the oldest things in this part of Oakdale," Joe added. "We have a neighborhood picnic here every summer."

"Yeah, but I like the idea of a Tastee Oasis," David said. "I could go for some right now. Have you ever tried its SuperFudge Delight? Or Triple Sundae with—"

A surprised look coming from Joe cut David off in mid-sentence.

"Sorry," David mumbled. "I kind of got carried away there."

"I know exactly what you mean," Wishbone told David. "I get that way about food myself."

"You *can't* cut down this tree," Sam protested.

"Sorry, young lady," Mr. King responded, "but the town says I can."

"Don't we get to have a say in this?" Joe asked.

"You tell 'em, Joe!" Wishbone cheered.

"You people already had a chance to make your feelings known," Mr. King responded.

"What do you mean?" Joe asked.

Mr. King walked over to a sign lying face-down on the ground and picked it up, dusting off some dirt. "The town held a hearing at my request for a zoning change several weeks ago," he explained. "The town council even posted a sign. See? Since nobody spoke out against building a Tastee Oasis at the hearing, my request was approved."

"We come here all the time, but we never saw that sign," David said.

"That's right," Sam chimed in. "What's it doing on the ground like that?"

"Well, young lady, sometimes these things fall down. Accidentally, of course." Mr. King tossed the sign back onto the ground.

"Nobody had a chance to see that sign," David objected. "That's not fair."

"That's not my problem," Mr. King snapped. "Why don't you kids get off my property." He walked toward them, coming to a stop right on top of Wishbone's sock.

Wishbone dashed forward. "Hey, mister, why don't you get off *my* property!" He tugged at the sock with his teeth until Mr. King moved off of it. "Hey!" Wishbone complained. "You stretched it all out. You've made a real mess of it."

"Come on," Joe said to his friends. "Let's go." He began to move away from the area.

David took Emily's hand. She grabbed the handle of her wagon with her other hand and followed behind him. After giving Mr. King one last, hard look, Sam turned and caught up with the others.

Wishbone trotted along beside Sam. As he passed

the large oak tree, he gazed up at its broad, leafy branches. "Here's looking at you, tree," Wishbone said sadly. The terrier picked up speed to catch up to the rest of his friends. "If you kids just put your brains together," he urged his friends, "you'll find a way to stop the construction."

"Let's think, guys," Joe insisted. "Among us, we should be able to come up with a way to stop this development plan."

Wishbone sighed. "Isn't that what I just said?"

Wishbone knew they didn't have much time to save the tree. *This problem needs a dogged approach and skill. Hmm . . . those were two of Odysseus's best qualities.* And just like Odysseus, Wishbone and his friends would have to take action.

Wishbone trotted alongside his friends through the deepening shadows. And he imagined himself once more as the warrior-hero Odysseus, trying to get his men home to Ithaca—in one piece.

CHAPTER FOUR

"Any sign of them?" a crewman called to Odysseus from the deck of the ship. Several weeks after leaving the island of the cyclops, they had anchored in a calm harbor. As Odysseus glanced at the ship from land, he could see several men making repairs. The rest of the crew hung around him on the beach. They were too worried to concentrate on their work.

"No!" Odysseus called back above the sound of the waves crashing at the shore. "I haven't seen anyone yet." He trotted up and down the beach. He listened carefully for sounds of his men, sniffing the air for their scent. It had been some time since he had sent a search party to explore the island. He was becoming concerned about their safety.

He did not have much longer to wait.

Eurylochus, an oarsman and member of the patrol, ran over a high sand dune, stumbling and falling. "Odysseus! Odysseus!" he shouted.

"What news have you, Eurylochus?" Odysseus

34

called. He could tell just by looking at the very upset young man that the news wasn't good—that, and the fact that Eurylochus was alone. Twelve other crew members had joined him on the scouting mission.

Eurylochus was gasping as if he had run a long way. Odysseus dashed over and placed a paw on him. Eurylochus calmed down.

Finally, he was able to speak. "Odysseus, it was horrible. Our men—they've all been turned into pigs!"

Odysseus cocked his head. "You mean they've been making pigs of themselves?" he asked. "That's not so unusual. We're all pretty hungry."

"No!" Eurylochus answered quickly. "They've been changed by magic into pigs. Real pigs."

"Pigs?" Odysseus repeated. "Curly tails? Snouts? Might someday be bacon?"

Eurylochus nodded grimly. The other crew members gathered around, shouting out questions.

Odysseus raised a paw. "Silence!" he commanded. "Let the lad speak."

Eurylochus took a few deep breaths, then started to tell his tale. "We found a palace ruled by a beautiful woman. She called herself Circe, ruler of the island we are on, Aeaea. She is a goddess with golden hair, fair skin, and sparkling green eyes, wearing a long, shimmering gown. With a great flashing smile, she invited everyone inside the palace. I alone was suspicious. Something about her didn't seem quite right."

"Smart boy." Odysseus nodded. He had been in similar situations himself.

"I decided to hide in the bushes until everyone

had gone inside," Eurylochus continued. "Then I looked into the windows and saw Circe work her magic spell. She gave the men food and drink. Then, with a touch of a wand, she turned them all into pigs!" Eurylochus covered his face with his hands, remembering the horrifying change that had taken place.

Odysseus shook his head. "Can't let those guys out of my sight for a minute," he said.

Eurylochus pulled himself together and finished his story. "They sit in their sty," he said sadly, "rolling in the mud, just like other pigs."

Eurylochus had finished telling his story about how the men had been bewitched. Odysseus immediately slung his bow across his back and snatched up his arrows, and his silver sword. "Lead me to where Circe is," he said.

Eurylochus's eyes widened in horror. "Don't do it—I beg you! How can we fight against the goddess's magic powers?"

"I will not abandon my men to this fate, but I will also not risk any more lives." He turned to his crew. "If I don't return by tomorrow morning, you will know that I have failed. If that happens, set sail and get yourselves home to Ithaca with my blessing."

Odysseus headed inland. He thought about the best way to battle a sorceress, a witch. *Those sorceress types always have some trick up their sleeve.* Leaping over small branches and ducking under trees, his every sense was alert to possible danger.

Suddenly, his ears twitched at the sound of a breaking twig. *Yes!* There, up ahead—someone was coming toward him. He crouched low, his belly to the ground. He gripped his sword in his teeth and waited to see who it was.

As the figure made his way through all the thick foliage, Odysseus recognized him immediately—and also realized that it was not a man. It was the messenger god Hermes, who had been a good friend to Odysseus in the past. Odysseus hoped the god would be a friend to him now, too.

"Hello," Hermes greeted Odysseus warmly. "What are you doing here? Never mind. I can guess where you are going—to Circe's palace, to rescue your men."

How does he know that? Odysseus wondered. *Oh, right . . . that all-knowing, all-seeing thing the gods do. If I had that skill, I'd be up on all the latest news, too.*

Before Odysseus could reply, Hermes gave him a warning. "I wouldn't do it if I were you, friend. Circe is a goddess herself, as well as a powerful sorceress. She'll be tough to outsmart."

It's never a good sign when even a god is nervous about what you're about to do, Odysseus thought. Still, he knew what action he must take. "I know the way is risky," Odysseus said, "but I cannot leave my men without at least trying to save them."

Hermes looked thoughtfully at the warrior-hero. "I admire you, Odysseus. For your loyalty and concern, I will help you." The god reached into the ground and yanked out a small plant by its roots, then handed it to Odysseus. "This is a special herb that will protect you from Circe's magic potions. The rest is up to you. If you manage to survive and win her affection, Circe can be a powerful ally and a good friend."

That's a pretty big "if," Odysseus couldn't help

thinking. But he knew that Hermes was trying to help. Odysseus wagged his tail in thanks. "Nice chatting with you, Hermes, but I gotta go. My men need me."

Odysseus bounded through the trees until he came to Circe's palace. Its large gray-stone walls rose up from a small hill in the center of a clearing. *Nice,* Odysseus thought, gazing at the fancy turrets and lush gardens. He walked out from the protection of the woods and sniffed the air. He caught the smell of wild creatures nearby, but he couldn't see them.

Come out, come out, wherever you are. He trotted across the clearing and scrambled up the steps to the massive front door of the palace. Suddenly, out of nowhere, savage beasts appeared. Mountain lions, wolves, tigers—with sharp claws and sharper teeth—surrounded him, yet not one snarled, raised a claw, or bit. All were calm and as friendly as tame pets.

Whoa! This Circe must be some powerful sorceress to have these wild beasts under her control—and not a leash among them. Well, I shall not become part of her zoo.

Odysseus stood on the wide steps and called out, "Circe!" Instantly, the doors opened. The sorceress herself stood before him. Her long, golden braids glinted in the sunlight.

"Won't you come in?" Circe invited.

"Don't mind if I do," Odysseus replied.

Circe led Odysseus into a huge dining hall. His nails clicked on the marble floor. "Make yourself at home," she offered, nodding to a comfortable chair next to a long table made of oak.

Odysseus hopped up onto the soft pillow. He circled once, twice, three times, then sat down.

Circe watched him carefully. "You must be very thirsty," she said. "Let me go and get you something cool to drink."

Here it comes, Odysseus thought. *Magic-potion time.* "Yes, why don't you do that?" he responded.

She brought him a refreshing drink in a small bowl. When she walked away for a moment, Odysseus dropped the protective herb Hermes had given him into the liquid.

When Circe returned to the table, Odysseus smiled at her. *She doesn't know that I'm on to her plan,* he thought. *Well, she won't be smiling for very long.*

"Bottoms up!" Odysseus drained every drop from the bowl, then licked it dry. "Mmm-mmm," he said. "Got any more?"

Circe stared at him. Her eyes widened, shocked that her magic potion hadn't worked.

"What's the matter, Circe?" Odysseus asked. "Cat got your tongue?" He prepared himself for whatever her next move might be.

Circe clutched her wand and tried to point it at Odysseus, but he was too fast for her. Leaping from his chair, he knocked the wand out of her hand with his muzzle, sending it clattering across the floor. Then he gripped his sword in his teeth. Circe screamed as he held the weapon to her throat.

"Gotcha!" he growled.

"Who are you?" Circe shrieked. "*What* are you? No one I have ever come across has ever been able to get the best of me before!"

"That's because you've never met anyone like me before," Odysseus bragged. "I am Odysseus." To make sure she understood his power over her, he bared his teeth and growled.

Circe gasped. "Yes, of course, I should have known it was you," the sorceress said. "Your visit was predicted, and I have been looking forward to meeting you. Although," she added, glancing down at the sword at her throat, "I hadn't exactly imagined our first meeting would go like this. Please, can't we forget about the past and start over from scratch?"

Odysseus remembered what Hermes had told him—Circe could be a valuable friend and supporter. "Before I release you," the hero said, "you must make me a promise that you will not try to bewitch me ever again."

Circe rolled her eyes. "I promise by all that the gods hold dear, I shall never attempt to harm you or bewitch you again."

"You'd better not have had your fingers crossed," Odysseus warned as he released her.

Circe stepped away from him, her nose wrinkling. "Why don't you freshen up?" she suggested. "Then we'll have dinner and get to know each other."

Odysseus looked down at his matted fur, and torn and dirty clothes, evidence of battle and long months at sea. "I suppose I could stand some freshening," Odysseus said with a laugh. "This hero business can really make a mess of your wardrobe."

Circe rang a silver bell. Two of her lady servants appeared. They led Odysseus to a roomy chamber. One maid brushed him until his fur gleamed. The other servant laid out fresh clothes made of the finest fabrics.

When they were finished with Odysseus's makeover, he admired himself in a mirror. "Now, that's more like it," he said. "I do have a pedigree to uphold."

When Odysseus returned to the dining hall, Circe was sitting at the long oak table. It was set up for a feast. "Come eat," Circe suggested. "Here are many fine foods that you surely must have missed in all of your time at sea."

Odysseus gazed at the delicious banquet items. There were silver bowls filled with his favorite kibble, and platters piled with thick, meaty bones. But, alas, Odysseus had no appetite to eat. His ears drooped as he lay down at the foot of the table.

"What's wrong?" Circe asked. "Do you still suspect me of trickery? Have no fear. I am a goddess who keeps her word. I promised you that I would do you no harm, and I meant it."

"How can I enjoy what you offer when part of my faithful crew is still bewitched?" he asked the sorceress. "If you really and truly want to be friends, you must set them all free."

"Is that all?" Circe stood up. "Follow me." Circe walked through the halls of the palace, her wand held high. Odysseus trotted beside her. They went out to the animal pens. Circe flung open the gates of the pens and drove out the huge pigs, which only hours before had been Odysseus's shipmates.

Odysseus shook his head as he watched the beasts squealing and stumbling over one another. "Guys, guys, guys. Control yourselves."

Circe glanced over at him and giggled. "Sorry,"

she said, trying to control her laughter. "But they do look funny."

Odysseus's fur bristled. "These were warriors— adventurers. You've made them ridiculous."

Circe giggled again, and Odysseus let out a low growl in response.

"Don't worry," Circe said quickly. "I am turning them back to what they were before."

One by one, Circe touched each pig with her wand and dabbed them with oil. More swiftly than Odysseus thought possible, the bristling skin softened, the snouts disappeared, and four legs turned back into two. His crew were men once again. They rushed to Odysseus, thanking him, clasping his paw in heartfelt handshakes.

"You saved us, Odysseus!" a man shouted. "We knew you would!"

Odysseus noticed Circe watching his reunion with his crew. "Thank you, Circe."

She shook her head. "No, Odysseus, it is I who thanks you. It is not often I am reminded of loyalty humans can have for one another." She gazed at Odysseus and his comrades for a moment. Then she added, "Listen, Odysseus, why don't you go back to your ship and get the rest of your crew? Let's not leave anyone out of the feast."

Odysseus's tail wagged, and he leaped joyfully into the air. *Way to go, Circe! Hermes was right—if one can just get past Circe's bad habit of casting spells, she is A-okay.*

"Back in a flash," Odysseus promised. Without another word, he raced all the way back to the beach.

His shipmates at the harbor shouted a welcome when they saw their leader running toward them. They cheered loudly when he told them Circe was now their friend—and they were all invited to the palace to join Odysseus and their other shipmates.

Upon Odysseus's return to the dining hall, Circe waved a hand. Several servants appeared, carrying large silver trays loaded down with warm breads and roasted meats. "Feast, my friends," Circe declared. "You will need all your strength for the long journey yet to come."

Odysseus's nose twitched as he smelled all of the glorious aromas. But food would still have to wait. He needed to find out what Circe meant by her last remark. "Do you mean that we will have to overcome yet more obstacles on our voyage home to Ithaca?" he demanded.

"Have no fear, Odysseus," Circe told him. "I shall tell you what you need to know to make your travels safer. Now, go ahead and enjoy the banquet with your friends. Who knows when you will be able to relax and celebrate again?"

Odysseus knew the goddess was right. He needed the nourishing food and good cheer as much as anyone else. Tail wagging, he raced to a table set with platters piled high with ripe cheeses, juicy fruits, and big joints of meats of every description. He placed his front paws on the edge of the table and peered at the food. "Hmm . . . so many dishes, so little time. I'll try one from column A, and two from column B—Hey! Does this one come with a side salad?"

Finally, after everyone had taken second and even third helpings of food, the men settled in for the night. They formed a temporary camp site in the great dining hall. Circe and Odysseus left the palace for an after-dinner stroll. They walked along the beach, discussing the journey that lay ahead for the hero and his men.

"I will tell you the best route to take, Odysseus," the goddess promised. "How you handle the dangers will be up to you."

"I am not afraid of anything, Circe," Odysseus stated. "We have already met and defeated many an enemy. You'd be surprised what a man can do to survive when he longs to get home to his native land, and to see once more his beloved wife and son."

Circe shook her head. "You will face enemies like you have ever seen before." Circe went on to warn Odysseus about the Sirens. They were strange and beautiful women who had already attracted many a sailor to his death by their magical song and voices. But she also offered her new friend a solution: "Fill your crewmen's ears with wax so they cannot hear the magical songs. And if you yourself must listen"—she glanced at Odysseus—"as I know you must, be sure to have your men tie you securely to the mast of your vessel. No man can hear the Sirens and not be tempted to join them in their watery grave."

"Got it." Odysseus scratched behind his ear with his hind leg. This task didn't sound too difficult. "Ear wax and a leash. No problem. What's next?"

"The double terrors of Scylla and Charybdis." Circe frowned. "You will reach two mighty cliffs where these two monsters live. Scylla lives on one cliff, and at the bottom of the other lives Charybdis."

"Two terrors for the price of one? I'll take a dozen," Odysseus said happily.

"Of these two, Charybdis the whirlpool is the more dangerous," Circe cautioned him. "But if you time your voyage right and steer your vessel close to the other cliff, you may pass unharmed."

Odysseus gazed at the goddess through narrowed eyes. He knew there was more bad news to come. The challenge she described couldn't be that easy to deal with. "Cough it up, Circe. Who—or what—is Scylla?"

Circe shuddered. *Hate that,* Odysseus thought. *This Scylla must be really bad news to scare a goddess.*

"Scylla is a terrible snakelike, six-headed monster living in a cave high up on a cliff. As ships pass, she snatches men out of them with her razor-sharp teeth."

Odysseus gulped. "Uh . . . Circe, did did you say *six* heads?"

Circe nodded.

"Well, I guess the saying 'two heads are better than one' doesn't impress her very much. I know how to deal with her—I'll behead her six times!" Odysseus declared.

"I know you dislike the idea of running away from anything, but just this once—please try to do just that," Circe said.

"Okay, okay, I get your point," Odysseus agreed. Still, he didn't like the idea of having to accept that his situation was as serious as Circe said it would be. *There may be a way out of this yet,* he thought.

Circe studied the warrior-hero's face. "I have one last warning."

Wow! Odysseus thought. *This is getting to be some to-do list.* "Maybe I should be taking notes."

"You will pass the island of Helios, the sun god," Circe went on. "It is a beautiful paradise. Peaceful and calm. Try to sail past it to avoid temptation. If you drop your anchor there, you and your crew may find it difficult not to help yourselves to the god's herds. But do not—I repeat, *do not*—go anywhere near Helios's herds. The cattle on his island are sacred to the god and therefore must not be touched. If you do, you will be destroyed."

"Is that all?" Odysseus said. "Easy. Hands off the herd. And now," he added with a yawn, "I think it's time for this hero to get some shut-eye."

Circe laughed. "Amazing," she said. "I warn you of terrible dangers, yet you are so calm you can drift off to sleep."

"Hey, after a great meal like the one you fed us, a

few monsters don't seem so scary," Odysseus said. "Besides, naps are very high up on my list of favorite things to do."

With that, Circe left for her rooms at the palace. Odysseus curled up and went to sleep.

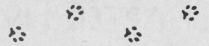

At dawn, Odysseus awoke and returned to the palace. He commanded all his men to take to the decks and cast off immediately. The crew bustled about the ship, and the oarsmen began rowing with rhythmic strokes. Circe stood on the shore, waving good-bye. As a final gift, she sent them sweet and steady winds to billow their sail.

"Thank you, Circe," Odysseus called. "Thank you for everything." He was grateful she had predicted the events of the next part of their long journey. He hoped Circe's warnings would allow him to better protect his men. One thing she did not mention was Ithaca. Would he and his men ever see their homeland again? *Fate is tough to beat, but doggone it, I am going to try!*

CHAPTER FIVE

Thanks to the strong and steady winds provided by Circe, the ship sped through the bright blue waters. Odysseus told his men of the dangers up ahead. His crew tied everything down on the ship from stem to stern—front to back. Then they allowed the winds to carry them along, steered by the sure hand of the helmsman.

Odysseus sniffed the air. "I smell land up ahead." *It must be the island of the Sirens.* He barked to get his crew's attention. "Comrades!" he announced. "As I told you earlier, Circe warned me of several dangers on this journey. We are about to meet our first, and should make preparations." He turned to his young steward and ordered, "Bring me a barrel of beeswax."

The young man stared at him. "Excuse me?"

"Do not question an order," Odysseus warned. "I know it's a strange request, but the reason will become clear soon enough."

The steward dashed belowdecks. Moments later,

he reappeared with a large barrel of beeswax, which they used for making candles. Steadying a hunk of wax on the deck with his paws, Odysseus took a small knife and cut off tiny pieces. Once he was done, he rolled the pieces between his paws. With the help of the sun, high overhead, the wax softened. Next, he told his men to form a line and then step forward one at a time.

Next, he stuffed the beeswax into his crew members' ears. Once he was finished, he went to his cabin and brought out several strong lengths of rope. He dropped them at the foot of the helmsman. With his paw, Odysseus gestured for the man to remove the ear wax for a moment so that he would be able to give the fellow instructions.

"You must tie me tightly to the mast," Odysseus instructed. "I alone shall listen to the singing of the Sirens. No matter how much I try to break free to join them, or how terribly I seem to suffer, you must ignore me. Wait until the island vanishes behind us. Then wait even longer than that—I don't know how far their voices carry. Wait until you see that I struggle no more and no longer seem to be bewitched by their singing. Then, and only then, untie me."

"Understood," the helmsman said, taking up the ropes.

Odysseus trotted over to the mast and stood patiently as the helmsman tied him up.

The helmsman checked and then double-checked to be sure that Odysseus was secured. Then he put the wax back into his ears and took his place at the helm.

"Okay, Sirens," Odysseus called out. "Ready when you are. Let's hear what kind of singers you are."

Suddenly, the sweet winds sent by the goddess Circe stopped, and all was calm. Too calm.

"I don't hear anything," Odysseus called. "What's the matter, Sirens? Suffering from a little stage fright?"

Then it came drifting across the water—the most beautiful, haunting voice he had ever heard. It was joined by another. The two singers harmonized a twin melody, two voices sounding like one, then like one hundred.

"I don't know that tune, but maybe if you hum a few bars . . ." Odysseus joked, trying not to be attracted by the glorious sounds. There were no words at first, just delicate and clear sounds. Odysseus's heart swelled with many different emotions—joy, sorrow, pride, and tenderness among them. All of his feelings were stirred by the Sirens' beautiful singing.

"I must see them!" he shouted. "I must know who these singers are!" He struggled against the restraining ropes, but his movements only made his bonds dig into his fur.

Then the singers began to sing words:

"Come close, come closer, Odysseus,
   Athena's pride, Ithaca's glory.
   Come close, come closer, Odysseus.
   Moor your ship so we may sing you a story."

"Untie me!" Odysseus commanded. "I am your captain. You must obey me!" He glared at his crew. *How dare they ignore me!* He snarled and barked, trying to get their attention, but no one responded.

50

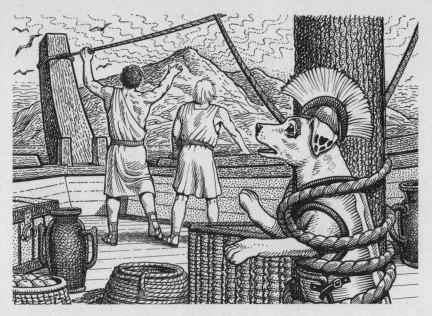

The Sirens continued to sing:

"Come close, come closer, Odysseus,
We alone know what you have gone through,
The losses and battles you have endured,
And the hardships that befall you."

Every word that the evil sea creatures sang pierced his heart. "Yes!" he wailed. "It's true! My loneliness is great—I long to return home, to my wife and son. And the burden of being a hero weighs heavily on me. I have to fight off the feelings of loneliness and fear in order to lead my men into battle. No one knows but you, Sirens!"

"Come close, come closer, Odysseus,
We have what you seek, what you yearn for.

Never has a sailor heard our song
Who hasn't become wiser . . .
Much wiser."

Every muscle in Odysseus's furred body strained against the ropes. He noticed the helmsman glance at him. Odysseus bared his teeth and made an effort to leap at him, only to be jerked back by the tight ropes. Then he sprang forward again, a low growl deep in his throat. The helmsman's face went white. Then he signaled to the men to row harder, faster than ever. The ship picked up speed. Odysseus howled into the sea winds as the Sirens's voices slowly began to fade.

Finally, their tempting songs were no longer heard. All Odysseus could hear was the slicing of the oars through the water and his own ragged breathing. When the helmsman saw that Odysseus no longer attempted to break free of his ropes, he untied the hero. They had passed the first danger Circe had warned them about. Odysseus gave the order that the men were now free to remove the wax from their ears.

"Well done, men," Odysseus told the crew. "One danger down, a few more to go."

He knew the next obstacle they would have to face on their journey would be far more difficult to survive. It was the dreaded watery passage over which the monsters Scylla and Charybdis ruled.

The ship traveled on. As they neared the passage, Odysseus called out to the helmsman, pointing, "Head for the narrow stretch of water between the two cliffs. And stay close to the cliff on the left."

"Aye, Captain."

Odysseus wasn't going to give up without a fight. He put on his armor and grabbed a spear in his teeth. He'd do his best to battle the beast called Scylla, no matter what Circe had said.

"That is *some* cliff!" Odysseus said as he peered up at the enormous cliff looming over them. He spotted a break in the smooth surface about halfway up. It was an enormous cave entrance, jagged and dark. A greenish mist floated out from the wide mouth of the cave. *That must be Scylla's lair,* he thought. He knew she hid inside, waiting for her next victims. Odysseus realized from this distance that he'd never be able to shoot her with one of his arrows.

He glanced to the other side of the ship. There, another cliff held them in. Odysseus watched in horror as the wild, spinning whirlpool known as Charybdis gulped down a great swallow of the sea, as deep and wide as several ships.

"Men!" he shouted above the thrashing waters. "Avoid this side! Steer close to the other cliff." Odysseus now knew Circe was right. *I must risk battling Scylla,* he realized. *Perhaps we will be lucky and lose no men to her monstrous six-mouthed appetite. But the ship will be destroyed for certain if we steer too close to Charybdis.*

The men shouted in fear as the swirling waters were sucked down, down, down, by Charybdis. Then, with a deafening roar, the waters exploded spray that seemed to spit all the way up to the heavens, splattering the cliffs, then crashing great waves down upon Odysseus and his crew.

"Stroke! Stroke!" Odysseus barked his orders as

the men screamed in terror. But the crew obeyed their captain courageously, straining their muscles, pulling like madmen on the oars.

Odysseus's whiskers twitched. A new scent! He glanced up at the cliff where the cave was.

"Scylla!" Odysseus gasped, his soaking-wet fur standing on end.

The ugly monster had twelve writhing legs, all of them dangling down out of the cavern. She displayed six long, scaly, serpentlike necks, upon each of which sat a hideous head. Each head had a mouth containing a triple row of fearful fangs, all gnashing and drooling.

In a moment of lightning-quick speed, Scylla struck. With swiftness, the terrifying monster reached out and then snatched up six men, one for each of its gruesome, dripping mouths.

Odysseus wanted to battle the beast, but he knew he and the rest of his crew could not stop the ship. They did not dare try to rescue their fellow crew members, or they, too, would end up being sucked down by Charybdis, or more would be eaten by Scylla.

"Keep rowing!" Odysseus cried out to his crew, who were retreating in fright. "Harder! Put your backs into it!" He trotted along all the rows of oarsmen, nudging each one with his wet nose. He tried heroically to get their attention back to the rowing of the ship, and away from the horrific sight of the slobbering, munching monster.

What a sight it was. Odysseus's four legs trembled as he stared up at his lost men, the six victims dangling helplessly from Scylla's nightmarish mouths. He watched, almost frozen, as Scylla dragged them up the side of the cliff. Finally, she pulled herself and the men into her cavernous hideaway.

Witnessing the death of such faithful warriors shook Odysseus to his bones. But he had to continue with the voyage. There was no time to mourn. He was a captain, with a duty to his remaining crew to get them home safely to Ithaca. He held on to his heartfelt belief that, despite the unfavorable odds, they could still reach home.

Finally, captain and remaining crew were able to put a safe distance between themselves and the terrifying cliffs. They sailed into calmer seas. The immediate danger had passed. Yet more physical threats certainly lay ahead.

CHAPTER SIX

Odysseus's mournful crewmen rowed silently through the water. Odysseus, too, felt the heavy grief of losing six more members of his proud crew. First he had been robbed of some of his faithful followers by the one-eyed cyclops, and now by the six-headed Scylla. *It's up to me as captain to make sure that this ship stays on course,* Odysseus reminded himself yet again.

He shook his furred body, as if to shake off the sadness of what had already happened in the many years they had spent sailing home after their victory in battle at Troy. He thought of his Penelope and his son, Telemachus. What dangers had they run into?

He shook his body again. Then he trotted between the oarsmen's benches, speaking words of hope, making jokes, and trying to lighten the dark mood.

Suddenly he raised his nose high in the air. His whiskers twitched. He caught the scent of land not far off. *We must be nearing the island of Helios, the sun god,* he thought. *It's the island Circe warned me to avoid.*

"Land!" the navigator shouted.

Odysseus could sense the ripple of excitement crackling through the crew. He glanced around. *Uh-oh. These guys are cheering up just* thinking *about dry land. It's going to be my unpleasant task to give them the bad news.* He shook his head. *We warrior-heroes get all the fun jobs.*

Odysseus leaped onto the platform at the front of the ship. "Shipmates! I know you are tired. But Circe warned me that we should not attempt to land on this island. You must steer away from its shore."

The men stared at him.

Well, that announcement went over big. "We will find nothing but trouble there," Odysseus added, hoping the crew would see the wisdom of his order.

Eurylochus stood. "Captain," he said, "I think I can speak for the entire crew. We are falling asleep at the oars. Our muscles ache, our hearts are heavy. And you tell us not to land?"

Odysseus watched the men speak quietly among themselves and then nod their heads. He agreed with them, but he also knew that landing would place them into great danger.

"Let us land!" someone cried from the back.

"It's getting late," Eurylochus pointed out. "We want to sleep on solid ground."

"Aye!" several voices hollered.

Odysseus knew that these men couldn't take any more. Otherwise, they would never try to change his mind about an order. His heart went out to them.

"All right," he agreed finally. "But you must all make me a promise—you will not go anywhere near the sun god's herds of cattle. No matter how hungry you are, you will not touch them."

"We promise!" the men shouted out as one.

Odysseus scanned the coastline. "There," he said, pointing. "I see a bay in which to anchor the ship. All hands, prepare to land."

Quickly, the men steered the ship into the bay, threw out the anchor, and set about getting ashore. Odysseus sniffed the air, wondering if giving in to his crew would land them in even hotter water.

Sleep came quickly to the tired travelers. While they slept, however, fate struck again, in the form of a powerful storm. Strong winds whipped up the waters and rain poured down. Luckily, the men had set up a temporary covered shelter and were able to stay dry and warm.

"It doesn't look as if we'll be leaving anytime soon." Odysseus told his disappointed crew the bad news the next morning, after he had taken a walk outside the tent. He shook his body, spraying water from his fur.

Odysseus worried as the days of waiting stretched out to five full weeks. *When it rains, it pours,* he thought, as the torrential downpour finally ended, only to be replaced by hurricane-force winds. He admired his crew's attempts at keeping up their spirits. The waters were too rough for fishing, and the simple diet of nuts and berries was getting old.

I could really go for a nice meaty bone just about now, Odysseus thought, his stomach rumbling. *I'd even settle for some beef-flavored potato chips! How much longer will the crew be able to stop themselves from taking the sun god's herd of animals for much-needed food?* he wondered. *Time to do some serious begging with the gods.*

Odysseus trotted off into the island's interior, searching for a spot protected from the bad weather. The wind was so strong that it nearly knocked him off his four feet. After a while, he came to a grove of thick, tall trees. Once inside their protective circle, the warrior-hero lowered his nose to his front paws in prayer. "Oh, great and mighty gods, enough already with the rain and the wind. Just tell us what you want us to do, and we'll do it! Please, just lighten up in the weather department, okay?"

Odysseus sniffed the air. *I hope they heard me. I wonder . . .* He broke off in a big yawn. *I can wonder later. Right now I could use a nap.* Odysseus circled three times and then lay down. *Why am I so sleepy? Could this be the work of some god?* As his eyes shut, he decided not to worry about it.

Odysseus awoke with a start. *That smell! That delicious scent!* His mouth watered and his tail wagged. *Barbecue!*

Then his heart thumped hard in his furred white chest. *Oh, no!* There could be only one explanation for the wonderful smell that made his whiskers tingle. *My crew must have broken their promise and raided the sun god's sacred herds.*

Odysseus raced back to the temporary camp. He was horrified to see his men feasting on the forbidden food. *We're in big trouble now!*

"What have you done?" he said furiously. He now knew for certain that the gods had deliberately sent him to sleep. If he had returned to his men sooner, they never would have disobeyed him. *Fate has once again worked against me and my men.*

"Don't be angry, Odysseus," Eurylochus begged. "We took great care to satisfy the gods. We gave them many thanks and special offerings before we roasted our meal."

"You disobeyed a direct order! Even worse, you have caused trouble so serious that there is nothing we will be able to do to correct it." Odysseus shook his head sadly. "It isn't my anger you need to worry about. We must leave this island immediately and hope that the gods don't notice what has happened." *As if they wouldn't,* Odysseus thought.

The winds died down to a whisper. *Great,* the hero thought. Now *you decide to clear up. A little late, don't you think?* But he knew better than to appear ungrateful. He figured he and his crew were in enough trouble already.

The men quickly returned to the ship, raising the sail, settling onto their rowing benches. Odysseus nervously paced the deck, his nails clicking on the wooden planks. *I don't like this,* he muttered, gazing up at the crystal-clear skies. *I don't like this at all. It is too peaceful. . . . I know the gods are angry.*

The ship sped away from the island, and soon the captain and his crewmen were sailing in open seas. Odysseus sensed a change in the air. He glanced up and saw the dark storm clouds gathering directly overhead. *Uh-oh,* he thought immediately. *I knew it was too good to be true.*

Crack! A blinding thunderbolt shot through the clouds and shattered the mast.

"Zeus, the king of all gods!" Odysseus exclaimed. "He sent his thunderbolt as punishment!"

Men screamed as the huge mast toppled. *Crack!* Another thunderbolt—this one hit the body of the ship. Odysseus was knocked off his paws as the ship buckled and split in two! The wooden deck above him burst into flames. He heard the cries of his crew as they were thrown into the violently churning waters. He caught the rigging in his teeth and held on tightly.

Crack! Crack! More thunderbolts, hurling the few men who still clung to the boards of the deck into the water. They fell directly on top of those who bobbed in the sea. The violent storm smashed apart what was left of the ship.

Odysseus straddled a heavy piece of deck and set up a crooked mast. He snagged a piece of sail that floated by him with his teeth and tied it securely to the mast. He tried to paddle back to his crew, but the powerful waves washed him farther away from the doomed ship. He watched its proud and mighty bow tip, then sink into the inky-black water. He no longer heard the cries and shouts of his crew. For them, the long, difficult journey was over.

Hours passed. Maybe even days. Odysseus shivered in the cold, damp air. His makeshift raft bobbed unsteadily on the waves. The shredded sail was barely able to trap the slightest bit of wind.

"Okay, this is no longer my idea of a good time," Odysseus said in a tired voice. His wet fur was matted, and the drying salt from the water made the pads of his paws sore. "I'm stuck out here all alone on a rickety pile of logs. I like my trees vertical."

He gazed out at the vast sea before him, which seemed endless.

"The situation has gotten so bad that I'm actually talking to *myself,*" Odysseus said. "How much worse can it get?"

Uh-oh, he thought, as he noticed the sea beginning to churn. *Famous last words.*

With a deafening roar, the waves whipped up in a frenzy, crashing down on Odysseus. He shook furiously, spraying water everywhere. Odysseus trembled in fear as he watched a wall of water rise high in the air. But instead of smashing down onto him, splintering his raft and sending him to a watery grave, the wave kept growing—and growing—until it formed itself into the face of a man.

"Wow!" Odysseus gasped. "That guy's big. And green. And scaly. Hmm . . ." he added, as he sniffed, "and he smells like fish."

"I am Poseidon, god of the sea," he boomed.

As if I couldn't figure out that one, Odysseus thought. He stood up as tall as he could and addressed the god. "I am Odysseus, warrior-hero."

"I know who you are," Poseidon declared.

Right. I keep forgetting about that all-knowing power these gods have, Odysseus scolded himself. "I've heard a lot about you, too," Odysseus said. "If what I've heard is true, I think I'm in big trouble."

"You have angered me greatly," Poseidon said. "You did harm to my son, the cyclops, Polyphemus."

"That's true, Poseidon," Odysseus admitted, "but he asked for it. Look at it from my point of view. I mean, the guy tried to eat me! And he had several of

my comrades as between-meal snacks. Is that any way for a god's son to treat his guests?"

"How dare you speak to me that way!" Poseidon declared. "That's another thing I've never liked about you, Odysseus. You seem to think you can do anything you want, no matter what the gods and the weather conditions say."

"I'm just trying to do my best," Odysseus said.

"Enough!" Poseidon's voice had such power that it billowed out Odysseus's sail, making his raft speed across the water.

"I'm sorry," Odysseus called. "Look, I don't mean to be paddling in your pond. I just want to get home so that I can be with my wife, Penelope, and my son, Telemachus."

"Then I hope you can swim!" The night sky crackled with thunder as a lightning bolt split Odysseus's raft into splinters.

"Mayday! Mayday! Abandon ship! Hero overboard!" Odysseus leaped into the water. Poseidon laughed so hard his huge shoulders shook. The movement made the ocean swirl into violent, churning waves. But the sound of the god laughing behind him only urged Odysseus on.

I refuse to allow the ocean to swallow me up, not when I have come so far and survived so much already. He dog-paddled furiously. Miles up ahead he was able to see land on the horizon.

Coughing, sputtering, and tired to the bone, Odysseus finally crawled onto dry land and collapsed. *If I were a cat, I would have used up several of my nine lives by this time.*

Then he sprang to his feet and shook the water from his fur. "But I'm not a cat," he declared to the misty fog. "I'm Odysseus, and I'm in the home stretch now. Not even Poseidon can stop me!"

Now, if I could only figure out where I am. He sniffed the air, but the fog was so thick all he could smell was dampness. *I'll start over again in the morning. Right now all I want to do is curl up and sleep.*

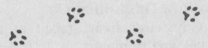

"Okay, now where am I?" When Odysseus awoke the next morning, the thick fog still lay over the land. "What new dangers will I find here? What strange people?" He yawned and stretched his four legs, stiff from the long swim the night before. He noticed a shepherd approaching him. *At least, I think it's a shepherd,* he thought. *But, for a shepherd, he's well dressed.*

Although the boy wore shepherd's clothing, Odysseus could see that the lad's knee-length shirt was finely woven, his sandals were of a golden color, and the face looked sort of familiar.

Keep on your paws, Odysseus reminded himself. *Something about this fellow makes me wonder if he's a god in disguise. They've been popping up pretty regularly.*

"Greetings, friend," Odysseus called. "You are the first native I've met. I have been traveling for many years and have suffered a lot. I hope you will help me."

The shepherd stopped in front of Odysseus, and Odysseus lowered his head to meet his front paws in a deep bow. He figured the show of respect couldn't hurt—it might even help.

"You see? I kneel before you as I would before a god." *Just in case you are one,* he thought. *I'm not taking any chances.* "And I beg you to tell me where I am, and who lives here. I have just washed up upon your shore and I am lost."

The shepherd gazed at Odysseus and grinned. Then he said, "You must come from very far away, indeed, not to recognize this place, for we are known all the way to Troy. This is Ithaca."

Ithaca! Odysseus's heart raced at hearing the name of his beloved homeland. *Can it be true? Have I finally come to the end of my journey?* Despite his joy, he knew not to give his true identity to this boy—or to anyone else, for that matter—until he knew what was going on at home. For ten years he had fought in the Trojan War, and he had spent another ten years trying to reach home. He had been gone a long time, and he had no idea how things might have changed.

"So tell me, stranger," the shepherd continued. "Who are you, and where did you come from?"

Think fast, Odysseus told himself. *Come up with a cover story, quick.* "You know, I believe I *have* heard of Ithaca, even as far away as my hometown, on the island of Crete. I'm something of a fugitive now—on the run. You know, wrong-place, wrong-time kind of thing. But I promise you, those who accused me have the story all wrong."

The shepherd began to laugh. As his shoulders shook in merriment, to Odysseus's surprise the boy began to grow taller! In front of Odysseus's amazed eyes, the shepherd changed himself into a lovely, gray-eyed woman.

"Athena!" Odysseus cried.

"Yes," the goddess of wisdom replied. "And I am glad to see that you have lost none of your cleverness." She laughed and looked affectionately at Odysseus. "You and I are old pros in the arts of trickery and careful planning."

Odysseus was overjoyed at seeing the goddess. Athena favored him, and he knew that at last he would have some help in discovering what still lay ahead for him. At least, he hoped she would help him. *You never can be too sure with these gods and goddesses. They are an unstable group.*

Odysseus knew how much importance all the gods placed on ceremonies and signs of respect. He knelt down before Athena again, even lower this time. "Goddess Athena, I fall before you and ask for mercy. I have been aided greatly by the gods, it is true, but I

have also suffered at their hands. Please, use no cruelty or tricks. You are looking at one tired hero." *Dog-tired, in fact,* he thought.

"Get up, Odysseus." Athena smiled at him. "I have nothing but your best interests in my heart."

Odysseus scrambled up on all fours. "Then I must ask you a question," he said. "Where were you during these many years I have struggled to reach home from my war victory at Troy, in the east?"

"Sometimes there is only so much even a goddess can do," Athena explained to him. "And remember, you angered some very powerful gods. That put me in a very difficult position."

"So tell me, Athena." Odysseus sat back on his haunches and gazed up at her. "Am I truly home, or is this yet another detour before I can make it back to the land and the family that I love with all my heart?"

"After all you have been through, I understand your caution, Odysseus," Athena replied. "But, yes, I assure you, this is your beloved Ithaca."

With a wave of her hand, she made the fog lift. Odysseus could see the hills of his youth on the horizon. There was the familiar pathway leading from the beach. Even his favorite tree still stood as it had on the day he left for the long war in Troy.

"I confess, it was I who covered the land with mist," Athena continued. "You needed to arrive home unseen, and it was important that I be the first one to greet you. Many things have happened here since you have been gone."

"I'll bet," Odysseus replied.

"Sit down," Athena commanded. "You are not going to like what I have to tell you."

Odysseus recognized an order when he heard one—he hadn't aced obedience school for nothing. He sat and waited for Athena to continue.

"For the past three years, your home has been overtaken by an unlawful and dangerous mob," Athena told him. "The members destroy all of your property. Even worse, they torment your son."

Odysseus's fur bristled with anger, but he tried to control himself. "Why don't they just steal all the treasures I have collected over the years and then be gone for good?" Odysseus asked the goddess.

"These men all hope to marry your dear wife, Queen Penelope," Athena replied. "They urge her to say you are dead because you have been gone twenty years. And they insist that she marry one of them."

It took Odysseus a moment before he could respond. "Is Penelope safe? Is she all right?"

Athena took his paw in her hands and smiled. "Your loyal wife has managed to hold them off. However, she is powerless to remove them from the property. She is very upset at the way they have destroyed your home. She has also grown tired from their continuous fights and demands. She lives in constant fear for herself and for your son, Telemachus. Both she and your son miss you terribly. She is right to fear. Time is running out for her."

Odysseus sprang to his feet. He growled and barked in fury, his eyes ablaze. "We must rid my palace of these violent men—these suitors—who take advantage of my lady's goodness and my absence in order to satisfy their greed." He looked at Athena with affection. "Thank you for delaying my entrance into the city. I would surely have walked straight into trouble without your help."

Athena's gray eyes glittered with pride and approval. "The trouble at hand will not be yours, my hero. Of that I have no doubt. Now, let me disguise you as a beggar so that you may arrive unknown and be successful in putting together a plan of action."

With another wave of her hand, the goddess then covered Odysseus in rags and gave him a beggar's bowl to carry. She aged him and matted his fur, covering him in grime. When she was finished, he looked like an old, weak beggar.

"My son, Telemachus," Odysseus said. "How is he? He must be grown by now."

"He is a young man to be proud of, Odysseus," Athena assured him. "In fact, I sent him away to better protect him. There has been a plot brewing among the suitors for your wife's hand. The plan, spearheaded by Antinous, is to murder your son on his return home. Have no fear. I shall escort him safely back to you unharmed. Now go," Athena ordered. "Go into the woods, where you will meet one of your loyal servants, Eumaeus, whose job it is to care for the pigs raised at your palace. He will give you a place to stay in safety until you are ready to make your move. I'll bring Telemachus to you in your hideout."

With that, the goddess vanished.

Well, I finally made it home, Odysseus thought as he trotted into the woods. *But there are obstacles still to overcome. In fact, the hardest battle will be to keep my temper and wait until the time is right to act. I must keep a clear head, no matter how much anger threatens to cloud my thinking. That will be the biggest challenge I have ever faced.*

CHAPTER SEVEN

Wishbone poked his nose out from underneath the kitchen table. "Hey, guys, I think that I've been pretty patient. You've all had your dinner, so where is mine?"

Wishbone wove in and out among the chairs, looking up at David, Sam, and Joe. "Helllooo! Aren't you forgetting something? Like feeding the dog?"

No one glanced down.

Wishbone sat and scratched himself behind the ear. "Okay. Next line of attack." Wishbone crossed over to Ellen, who stood talking on the phone. He reached up and placed both paws on her legs.

Ellen shooed him away. "Not now, Wishbone. I'm busy."

"Hmm . . . Now what?" Wishbone glanced around the kitchen. "I know. I'll use visual aids." He trotted over to his food bowl, his nails clicking on the linoleum floor. "Here I am! Looking cute and hungry. Somebody? *Anybody?*"

"Do you think we'll be able to save the old tree?" Sam asked. She got up and brought her dinner plate over to the sink.

"We can try," Joe told her.

"The real problem will be time," David said. "We don't have much of it."

"We don't have much in my food bowl, either," Wishbone complained. "Why don't we solve that problem first? Huh? Okay?"

Sam glanced over at Wishbone. "Oh, Wishbone, are you hungry?" she asked. "We're so caught up worrying about all the trees that we forgot all about you." She grabbed a bag of kibble from the counter and then poured some into Wishbone's food bowl.

"Thanks, Sam," Wishbone said. "You're my hero."

"Are you sure that's our only choice?" Ellen said into the phone. "What about the tree-preservation law? . . . I see. Okay. Thanks a lot, Betty. I'll talk to you tomorrow." She hung up the phone and then joined the kids at the table.

"That didn't sound very encouraging, Mom," Joe said cautiously.

Ellen shook her head in frustration. "What Mr. King is doing is perfectly legal. His construction plans were all approved by the town zoning board. Unfortunately, that new law to protect the large trees doesn't take effect until next month. It looks like Mr. King got his friends down at city hall to rush his request through before the law goes into effect."

"But can't we do *anything*?" Joe asked.

Wishbone rubbed his head against Joe's knee.

"Sure we can, Joe!" He wagged his tail. "So what's the first order of business?"

"Well, the only thing we could do is get a restraining order," Ellen explained. "That way, Mr. King wouldn't be able to cut down the tree until we brought the subject before the town council."

"What good would that do?" Sam asked.

"Well, if we collected enough signatures against cutting down the tree, we might be able to get some kind of special protection for the old tree," Ellen told them.

"Yoo-hoo!"

Wishbone darted back under the table at the sound of Wanda Gilmore's voice. Sometimes Wanda objected to Wishbone digging in her garden. *Let's see,* he thought, *when was the last time I was over there? Not anytime today! So she can't be coming over to complain about me.*

"Come on in, Wanda," Ellen called out.

Wanda, the Talbots' next-door neighbor, hurried into the room waving a newspaper clipping. "Here's that article about the old tree I wrote some years ago for the Oakdale Arbor Society newsletter," she announced. "I'm sure this will change the minds of the members of the town council."

Ellen smiled and took the clipping. "I'm afraid our only chance is a petition drive."

"If it's a fight the developers want, we'll give them the fight of their lives," Wanda said firmly. "I've organized plenty of petition campaigns in my day. Nobody's been able to withstand a Wanda Gilmore petition drive yet. I have a perfect record."

Wishbone rolled over three times. Then he sat up and barked. "Sounds like a plan!"

The next day, Wishbone, Wanda, and Sam were set up at a table at the front entrance of the library where Ellen worked. They were collecting signatures for their petition, and handing out flyers.

Wishbone placed his front paws on the table, nosing the stacks of papers. "Let's see . . . Do we have enough petition sheets?"

"Wishbone, stop!" Wanda said. She pulled the petition pages closer to her side of the table.

Sam laughed and leaned over to scratch Wishbone's head. "He's just trying to help," she said.

Wishbone wagged his tail. "That's right! Put me to work. I want to save that tree as much as you do. I mean, trees are way up there on my top-ten list."

Wishbone circled the table. He noticed Sam's backpack leaning against a table leg. It was holding down a stack of flyers. "I know! I'll hand out flyers." Wishbone tugged a few of the papers out from under the backpack with his teeth. He trotted back and forth near the table, waving the papers. "Extra! Extra! Read all about it! Save our trees!"

A girl about Sam's age came over and bent down and patted Wishbone on the head. "What do you have there, boy?" She took the flyer from Wishbone. She quickly looked over the page and then hurried over to the table.

Wishbone watched her sign a petition with satis-

faction. "Now all I need to do is hand out a few thousand more of these and we should be set." He darted back to the stack and pulled some more flyers free of the backpack.

This time Sam noticed him. "Wishbone, what are you doing?" She reached down and took the flyers out of his mouth. "We have to hand these out."

Wishbone gazed up at her and cocked an ear. "What do you think I'm doing? Oh, I get it. I can't hand them out since I don't have any hands. Well, then I can *paw* them out. I just want to help!"

"Why don't you sit right here?" Sam instructed. "You can be on guard duty."

"I can do that!" Wishbone positioned himself directly in front of the table. "Hey, do I get a uniform? I'd look good dressed as a security guard. It would make me seem important. The blue fabric would go well with my fur." He gazed up at the table, but no one was paying any attention to him. "Oh, well, I guess it's plain clothes for me."

"Thank you, sir," Wanda said cheerfully, as a tall man finished signing a petition.

"Don't you walk off with that pen," Wishbone warned. "Not while I'm on the case."

The man laid the pen back on the table and gave Wishbone a couple of pats on the head. "Cute dog," the man said.

Wishbone gave him an approving nod. "That's what I like to see. Nice, law-abiding citizens, with great taste in dogs."

"How's it going?" Ellen asked as she came out of the library and joined them at the table.

"One hundred thirty-two signatures so far," Wanda announced proudly.

"And one set of paw prints," Wishbone added.

Ellen sighed. "We need thirteen hundred."

"Don't worry," Wanda said with confidence to Ellen and Sam. "I've got my friends from the Oakdale Arbor Society at the mall. Before we're through, we'll pull in the big numbers."

Suddenly Joe dashed up the stairs leading to the library, out of breath. Wishbone leaped to his feet, ready for action. "What is it, Joe?" he demanded.

"What is it, Joe?" Ellen said with concern.

"Mom! Mom! They've already started. We've got to do something—quick!"

Wishbone glanced at Joe's flushed face. "Uh-oh. Looks like trouble."

"Calm down, Joe," Ellen said, laying a hand on Joe's shoulder.

"Take a deep breath and start over," Wishbone instructed his pal.

Joe took in several breaths, then began again. "Bulldozer!" he said. "They've got a bulldozer, and they're starting to clear out all the trees. David's videotaping the whole thing."

"So they want to play rough," Wanda said with determination, rising from her seat. "Hold down the fort, Sam." She came out from behind the table and joined Joe. She tugged the brim of her straw hat. "Let's go take care of this right now."

Joe and Wishbone dashed down the broad library steps after her.

"Be careful," Ellen called.

"We will," Wishbone answered back.

"I'll meet you there," Wanda told them at the corner. "I have something I need to do first. You try to stop them, but don't do anything reckless."

Wishbone cocked an ear. "Who? Us? Never! Bold, maybe. Brave, definitely! But *rash?* No way."

Joe and Wishbone ran through the neighborhood until they came to the woods.

"I'll let David know that help is on the way," Wishbone said. He raced ahead, putting on speed. *Four legs really do come in amazingly handy when a guy is in a hurry.*

Up ahead, Wishbone could hear the loud, roaring sound of the bulldozer as it churned up the earth. He spotted David by the large tree, video camera in hand.

"Are you getting it all on tape?" Wishbone asked.

David didn't answer, concentrating instead on videotaping the destruction of the area.

What a mess! Wishbone thought, as he glanced around. *I hope we're not too late.*

Wishbone could see how much damage had already been done as he leaped over fallen tree branches. Felled trees and uprooted bushes and shrubs were scattered all over. Piles of dirt towered above him.

Wow! he thought. *That bulldozer is a seriously powerful digging machine. You almost have to admire it.* Then he realized something terrible: *That bulldozer is digging up* my *territory!*

"Hey, you there with the bulldozer!" Wishbone shouted. "Nobody digs here but me!"

He was greeted only with a loud roar. Wishbone moved in closer. *This is one stubborn machine. Someone has to stop that guy.* Wishbone whipped his head back and forth, scanning the area. *And I guess that someone is going to be me!*

"I'm not kidding! Quit digging where you're not wanted! Now, don't make me say that again."

Still, the powerful teeth of the bulldozer sank into the earth, scooping up huge chunks of dirt.

"What's the matter?" Wishbone barked. "Aren't you listening?"

We have to stop this destruction somehow. No matter what it takes!

Wishbone eyed the bulldozer. He couldn't help but notice that machine and dog were not evenly matched.

"I am one dog against all odds!" Wishbone said, as he immediately leaped into the scoop of the bulldozer's jaws. "I've got you right where I want you. Whoa—"

Wishbone lost his balance as the jaws suddenly lifted high into the air. He peered over the edge of the scoop and discovered that the ground was now a very long way down.

"Uh-oh," he muttered aloud. "I think that I'm in big trouble."

Odysseus got himself into tight spots just like this. But somehow he always managed to land with all four feet firmly on the ground.

CHAPTER EIGHT

Odysseus trotted through the woods. Memories filled his head with every step he took. "Great digging over there," he remembered. "And I think I should still have a few bones buried somewhere in that direction."

But all that would have to wait until he rescued his wife and son from the invasion by the suitors.

"How dare those lawless men think they can just take over my palace and terrorize my family," he fumed. "They may think I'm dead, but anyone can see that I am not!"

Finally, Odysseus came to a clearing at the edge of a large farm. A roughly built hut with a thatched roof stood a few yards away.

"Where did this come from?" Odysseus wondered. "It wasn't here when I left." Of course, he knew much had changed since he had first set sail some twenty years ago to fight the war in Troy.

Odysseus sniffed the air. *I can smell pigs nearby.* In

the doorway of the hut sat an old, white-haired man fixing his leather sandals. Odysseus settled back on his haunches and watched the servant work.

Why, it's my faithful servant, Eumaeus! Odysseus realized. As swineherd, it was Eumaeus's job to tend the pigs. *But why is he living among the animals he takes care of?* Odysseus cocked an ear. *Well, I won't find out anything by just sitting here. And Athena said he was one of the servants I can trust. Time to try out the beggar act.*

Odysseus approached Eumaeus. "Hello, there, friend," he called.

Eumaeus glanced up. "Yes, old man?" the servant said. "Can I help you?"

For a moment, Odysseus was startled at being called "old man," since Eumaeus was by far the older of the two. Then he remembered his disguise. "I've been traveling a long distance, and I could use some water," Odysseus said.

Eumaeus gave Odysseus a long gaze. "From the looks of you," he said, "you could probably do with a meal, as well. Come inside, old man. Let me give you some food, and you can rest."

"For that I would be most grateful, indeed," Odysseus said, pleased by the servant's kindness to a poor beggar. Odysseus followed Eumaeus into the hut.

"My lodgings are poor," the swineherd apologized. He made a cushion for Odysseus from his own bedding. Odysseus lay down on the pillow.

"So you live here among the pigs?" Odysseus asked. "That must be . . . handy. Living so close to work, I mean. No long commute."

Eumaeus snorted. "I built this hut because I could

no longer live at the palace. That used to be my home. But it has been overrun by the queen's suitors. Their behavior upsets me, and I'm not one to keep quiet when I see injustice."

"I know what you mean, friend," Odysseus told Eumaeus. He knew he needed to win Eumaeus's trust in order to have his confidence. "I'm the same way myself. Speaking openly has caused me problems in the past, also. This isn't how I normally look." He gazed at his matted fur. *Now, that's an understatement.*

Eumaeus eyed Odysseus curiously. "I could tell by your manners and by the way you carry yourself that you were not always poor, even though you are dressed as a beggar."

Uh-oh. Obviously, I still need to work the kinks out of my "wandering beggar" routine. Odysseus needed to steer the conversation toward the goings-on at the palace. He needed to know exactly what he might be walking into so he could be well prepared.

"You said you were troubled by the events at the palace. Like what?" Odysseus asked.

Eumaeus sighed. "It has been a long time since my master, the king, went to war far away, and still he has not returned," Eumaeus replied. "I would rather live among these pigs than among the mass of human swine at the palace."

So there are a lot of them. That's useful to know. "Sounds like your herd of pigs is better behaved."

Odysseus scratched behind his ear. *Could Athena have given me fleas to make my disguise complete?* he wondered. *That would be a little too much, even for her. Although she does have a good sense of humor.*

"Well, even with all your troubles, you have been very kind to me," Odysseus told Eumaeus.

"Why, I am just doing what is right," Eumaeus replied. "But enough of this talk. I have promised you a meal." He set a plate of food before Odysseus. "Eat, stranger," Eumaeus urged.

Odysseus didn't need to be told twice. He hadn't seen meaty bones like these since he had been at the banquet long ago on Circe's island. "I've always been a big fan of a good bone," he admitted, grinning at Eumaeus.

Odysseus noticed that the swineherd had offered him the best cuts of meat.

"May you be as dear to Zeus as you are to me for your kindness," Odysseus told Eumaeus.

"Enjoy, my new friend. I am happy to be able to offer such a meal to you."

Odysseus's tail wagged for the first time in quite a while. He was warm, he had a big bone to gnaw, and he was finally back on dry land—for good.

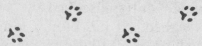

The next morning, Eumaeus awoke Odysseus at dawn. "I've made you some breakfast," the swineherd told him, holding out a bowl of tempting food. "I am off to tend to the herds."

Odysseus stood and stretched all four legs, shaking off his warm blanket. His ears pricked up at the sound of footsteps outside. "Someone is approaching," he said.

Before Eumaeus had a chance to check, Telemachus

stepped through the doorway. The swineherd was so startled by the arrival of the young prince that he dropped the bowl, which clattered to the floor. He rushed over to Telemachus as if he were his own son, throwing his arms around the young man in a warm hug.

"You've returned home safe and sound from your trip!" Eumaeus cried. "I never thought you would come back alive from Pylos. Come in!" he added, as he led Telemachus to a crudely built wood chair.

The emotion of seeing his son again was so much for Odysseus that he didn't trust himself to speak, so he stayed silent. *That's my baby boy all grown up,* Odysseus thought as he gazed at the young man. *But I cannot tell him who I am—at least, not just yet. Not in front of Eumaeus. I'll have to find a moment alone with him.*

Telemachus smiled warmly at the servant. Then he glanced over at Odysseus, who sat by the fireplace. "May I speak plainly, Eumaeus?"

Eumaeus nodded toward Odysseus. "I believe this man can be trusted. Please, what do you have to say?"

"I came to ask you what might be waiting for me at the palace," Telemachus said. "Do my mother's suitors wait in ambush? I know they plot against my life. You are the only man I trust to tell me the truth."

Odysseus shook his head, frustrated that he had to keep up his beggar's disguise. His fur bristled with anger over the idea that his son's life was in danger. Still, he kept silent.

"The suitors are too distracted by food and drink to have made serious plans against you," Eumaeus informed Telemachus. "But beware of Antinous, the ringleader of the whole group. He keeps trying to encourage the other men into action."

"Thank you for all the information." Telemachus looked over at Odysseus again. "Eumaeus, who is your visitor? I believe he is a stranger."

"He's a shipwrecked beggar," Eumaeus explained. "I was hoping to present him to you so you could protect and shelter him."

"Shelter?" Telemachus replied. "I wish I could offer that and more, but my home is not safe—neither for me nor for strangers. All I can offer is some clothing and a sword. That way, he can protect himself against the suitors if they choose to torment him for sport." Next, Telemachus addressed Odysseus. "Understand, friend, alone these men are all cowards, but as a pack, they become bullies."

Odysseus knew he had to respond, or his son would become suspicious. It would be rude for a beggar not to thank a prince. "I thank you for your offer. You and Eumaeus are both so kind that it breaks my heart to hear you both talk about these lawless suitors. But surely there must be those who can help you, my prince."

"If only there were," Telemachus replied. "But I see no end to this struggle unless my father returns, or my mother finally gives in and marries one of the suitors. And to her, that solution would be unthinkable."

Odysseus nodded. *So Telemachus and I are on our own in this matter.*

"Eumaeus," Telemachus said, "please go to my mother and tell her secretly that I have returned. I don't want her to worry. But don't tell anyone else, since there are so many plotting against my life."

Eumaeus patted Telemachus on the shoulder, then grabbed his cloak. "I'll be as quick as I can with this news," he promised. Then he left the hut.

Suddenly, Athena appeared in the doorway. She told Odysseus she was visible only to him. *Neat trick,* Odysseus thought, as he gazed at the radiant goddess. *I wish I could do that. It's a talent that would sure come in handy.*

"Now is the time, Odysseus," the goddess said in words only Odysseus could hear. "Before Eumaeus comes back, tell your son who you are. Together you will plot your victory over the suitors."

Athena clapped her hands, and Odysseus's beggar disguise melted away. His four legs lost their gnarled and bent shapes, returning muscles to their original straight and powerful form. His eyes sharpened and his whiskers were no longer stiff with dirt. His fur shone again, and fine clothes appeared on his back.

"That's much better," Odysseus commented with satisfaction. "That other outfit just wasn't me."

Telemachus fell to his knees in front of Odysseus. "Who are you?" the surprised young man asked. "Surely you are some god, to be able to change right before my eyes."

"No, I am not a god," Odysseus said gently. He reached out with his paw and placed it tenderly on Telemachus's cheek. "I am your father, Odysseus. I have come home at last."

Telemachus stumbled backward, terrified. "No mortal man could transform in such a manner," he

protested. "You can't be my father. You must be some spirit trying to trick me. One minute you were an old beggar, and now you look like a hero."

"Did I really look *that* bad?" *Well, Athena always does good work.* "You must believe me. I give you a solemn promise that I am indeed your father, Odysseus."

"But how—?" Telemachus's eyes were wide with wonder, obviously still trying to understand what he'd just witnessed.

Odysseus shrugged. "The make-over? That was the goddess Athena's handiwork. I can't take credit for it."

At that, Telemachus threw his arms around his father. For the first time in his whole life, Odysseus felt tears forming in his eyes.

"Tell me everything, Father," Telemachus cried. "How did you get here? And what took you so long to return? What—"

Odysseus stopped him. "I promise I will tell you the whole story later. Right now we have to make plans to rid our kingdom of the unwanted suitors."

"Father, I mean no disrespect," Telemachus said, "but there are a lot more of them than there are of us."

Odysseus laughed. "Don't worry, son. This old soldier still has plenty of tricks up his sleeve. Besides, I have friends in high places. The goddess Athena has already promised her help." He cocked an ear at Telemachus. "Think about it. With Athena on our side, do you think we still need more help?"

Telemachus smiled. "No. I think Athena knows what she's doing."

"Okay. Here's the plan. Go home and tell no one I am here. I will arrive at the palace wearing my beggar's disguise. You must do nothing to give me away—no matter how I am treated."

"Got it," Telemachus replied, with a sharp nod of his head.

Father and son spent the rest of the morning shaping their plan, until Eumaeus returned. Just before the swineherd entered the hut, Athena changed Odysseus back to his beggar's disguise. This time, Telemachus was much less shocked by the change.

"Welcome back, Eumaeus," Telemachus said. "I was just going. Bring this beggar to the palace tomorrow. I shall give him fresh clothing and sandals when he arrives. We will fix him up as best we can, provided the suitors let us."

Odysseus's eyes glowed with pride, listening to his son's commanding voice and cleverness. *Good! Quick cover story,* he thought with admiration. *That's my boy—a chip off the old block.*

"Till tomorrow," Telemachus said softly as he strode to the door.

"Till tomorrow," Odysseus repeated. *And what a day tomorrow is going to be.*

CHAPTER NINE

The next morning Eumaeus and Odysseus left the safety of the hut in the woods and went to town to the palace. The great warrior-hero was still dressed in his beggar's rags. "Just remember to be careful," Eumaeus cautioned. "Those suitors spell trouble—with a capital T."

They soon arrived at the courtyard outside the grand palace. Music flowed from the windows, and Odysseus cocked an ear. "I hear a party." Then he sniffed the air. The strong scent of roasting meat made his whiskers twitch. "I smell one, too."

Eumaeus sighed. "The suitors make merry from sun-up till sun-up. They stuff themselves with food, and they drink and fight all day and all night long."

"Well, I think it's high time I meet these party animals," Odysseus declared.

"I'm afraid you have no choice, friend," Eumaeus replied. "Telemachus wants to see you, and I believe he is inside with them."

So, at last, Odysseus put his four paws inside his own home for the first time in twenty years. But his arrival was not that of a triumphant warrior-hero, as he had always imagined it would be. Instead, it was in the form of a lowly beggar.

Evidence of the suitors' presence was everywhere. Furniture was overturned, broken, and thrown all over the palace. Stains discolored the once-plush carpets. "These guys are not at all housebroken," Odysseus commented, scanning the mess.

Odysseus heard shouts and laughter over the music that was coming from the banquet hall. He also heard the sharp sounds of smashing dishes. *Business as usual,* Odysseus suspected.

"You see why I never come here unless I am directly ordered to do so?" Eumaeus asked with a shake of his head. Together, the two entered the banquet hall, which was in even worse shape than the entrance court they had first passed through.

Telemachus stood at the far end of the hall. He spotted them immediately and waved them over. Dozens and dozens of men filled the room, eating and drinking and shouting. *They're spilling and breaking things and making pests of themselves,* Odysseus observed. *No doubt about it—these guys would all flunk out of obedience school.*

As the swineherd and the beggar made their way through the noisy crowd, many of the suitors gave them nasty looks.

Antinous, the ringleader of the failed plot to murder Telemachus, eyed them with hate. "You, there, swineherd!" Antinous shouted. "What do you mean by bringing this beggar to town? Don't we have enough wanderers already trying to help themselves to what doesn't belong to them?"

"You're a fine one to talk, Antinous," Eumaeus shot back at the ringleader of the suitors. "Whose plate is that you hold in your hands?"

Score one for Eumaeus, Odysseus thought.

Antinous pulled back his arm and threw the plate at Eumaeus. Luckily, Eumaeus ducked out of the way just in time.

"I don't answer to you, Antinous, or to any of your other scavengers." Eumaeus glared at the crowd of suitors. "In Odysseus's absence, I answer only to that man there." He pointed at Telemachus. "And, of course, to my queen, the good lady Penelope."

Score two for Eumaeus. Three times, and Antinous will be out.

"Enough!" Telemachus called out. "Antinous, I know you don't want me to waste a scrap of food on a hungry beggar when I could waste it on you."

"Your words don't scare me," Antinous sneered.

Odysseus hated the insulting way Antinous addressed his son. "Too bad your brains don't match your strength," Odysseus said before he could stop himself. "Then you'd realize that you and all these scoundrels will be punished for your actions here."

"Don't you dare speak to me that way, you lowly beggar!" Antinous shouted. He grabbed the nearest thing he could—a footstool—and threw it at Odysseus. The rest of the suitors burst out laughing.

Odysseus didn't run. Instead, he took the blow as best he could. His four legs trembled a bit, but he held his ground. He forced himself to fight back his anger. *Let's see,* he thought. *So far today, I've been kicked, insulted, and had furniture thrown at me. This isn't exactly the warm welcome I had expected.*

Odysseus could see his son struggling to resist the urge to help him. But he shook his head, hoping Telemachus would understand it as a signal to leave things be. *Now is not the time to fight,* Odysseus knew. *But believe me, this misbehaved group of bullies shall pay for all they have done.*

"You say another word to me," Antinous threatened Odysseus, "and I'll have you skinned alive."

That guy is as nasty as a cornered alley cat, Odysseus observed. Then a sudden murmuring rippled through the crowd. They all stared at someone who had just entered the banquet hall. Odysseus hopped on a nearby stool in order to be able to see. There in

the doorway, in a long, flowing gown, stood his own dear wife, Penelope. She wore an expression of fury on her face.

"What is going on down here?" she demanded to know. "I could hear you fighting up in my chamber. Attacking a faithful servant and a poor, defenseless beggar—it is shameful behavior, Antinous."

Odysseus's tail wagged as he gazed at his wife with admiration. She was so strong, so pure, that her natural goodness shone out of her. *There she is, the woman I have thought of year after year, island after island. I have imagined this moment for so long that it almost feels unreal to be standing in her presence.*

Penelope was still beautiful—even after all this time, and grief—although Odysseus recognized the traces of tears lining her face. Around him, the suitors ducked their heads and seemed to be embarrassed in front of the lovely queen.

"She must be really angry," Eumaeus whispered to Odysseus. "She never appears before the suitors, she dislikes them so much."

One of the suitors, Eurymachus, stepped forward. "Ah, Penelope, how beautiful you look today—more beautiful and more wise than all of the women of Ithaca."

Penelope gazed coolly at the heavyset, sweating man, his clothing stained with spilled wine. "No, Eurymachus. Perhaps that was true once, but any beauty I might have had vanished the day my dear Odysseus sailed away to war. And I do not need false words from any of you."

"If you would be reasonable and choose one of us

to be your husband, all the rest of us would go away," Antinous pointed out.

Penelope glared at Antinous, her eyes flashing with anger. "You claim you are all here because you wish to marry me, but what do you really do? You are wild, make messes, abuse my servants and my son. When noblemen come to court a noble woman, they bring gifts, they shower her with kindness, they bring their own food to the feasts. They don't eat her out of house and home!"

You tell 'em! Odysseus thought. He admired her ability to speak out so strongly to the suitors without losing her charm and nobility.

"Gifts?" Eurymachus repeated, then laughed. "Well, if all you're waiting for is a big pile of presents, I think we can manage that."

Odysseus noticed a tiny smile on Penelope's face. He knew she had no plans of marrying any of these creeps. Instead, she hoped to replace some of what they had taken from the household with her clever request for gifts.

I certainly married the right girl, Odysseus thought. *She has spent years confined by the rules of her position, yet she has still managed to keep the suitors at a safe distance.* He knew a lesser woman would crumble—but not his Penelope.

"Let's go get Penelope her treasures!" Antinous shouted. "Then maybe she will finally come to her senses and choose herself a new husband."

"After all, Penelope," Eurymachus warned, "none of us plans to leave the palace until you have married one of us."

"Don't forget, I have plans of my own." Penelope spun on her heel and walked out of the room, her ladies-in-waiting scurrying behind her.

"My gifts will be much better than yours will," Antinous bragged to Eurymachus.

"We'll just see about that!" Eurymachus shot back.

All around Odysseus, the suitors began to argue about who would present Penelope with the greatest treasures. He shook his head. *These guys are pitiful. They'll fight about anything.* The situation gave him an idea—a way to get the suitors out of the palace long enough so that he could put the first steps of his plan into action.

"These men shouldn't be wasting their time arguing," he said to Eumaeus in a loud whisper.

Odysseus wanted the suitors to think they were overhearing him accidentally. He knew that they would never take a suggestion from a lowly beggar.

He placed a paw alongside his nose, as if he were trying not to be heard. "I bet Penelope will favor whoever brings her the gifts first," he added. "The early bird catches the worm, after all."

Just as he hoped, Antinous and Eurymachus exchanged a quick worried glance, then dashed for the banquet hall's exit. A mad stampede of suitors raced toward the doors. They knocked over furniture and tripped over one another in their rush. In a matter of minutes, the only men left in the hall were Eumaeus, Telemachus, and Odysseus.

"I'm going to hurry back to the herd while the suitors are off gathering presents," Eumaeus told

Odysseus and Telemachus. "I know you'll be safe while the suitors are gone."

"Go take care of the pigs," Telemachus said. "This beggar and I will find plenty to talk about, I'm sure."

Odysseus's tail wagged as he added, "Oh, I think we can come up with some way to pass the time."

CHAPTER TEN

The moment after Eumaeus left the banquet hall, Odysseus and Telemachus sprang into action. "Quick!" Odysseus ordered. "We need to lock up all the weapons and the armor."

Telemachus set about the task with his father, pulling spears and swords down from where they hung on the huge palace walls. Odysseus leaped up and grabbed a shield, sending it clattering to the growing pile already on the floor. Grunting and straining, they carried the weapons into the storeroom, then locked the door and returned to the hall.

"But what do I tell the suitors if they notice what we've done?" Telemachus asked. He crossed his arms and gazed up and down the bare walls.

Odysseus sat and scratched his ear with his hind leg for a moment. "I know," he declared. "Tell them you were worried that someone might get hurt during the feasting and partying. Accidentally, of course," he added, with a sly grin.

"And if they question me further, I'll tell them the smoke from the torches along the walls was ruining the steel," Telemachus suggested.

Odysseus patted Telemachus. "Clever lad. Now, off you go to bed. We've got a big day ahead of us. But first, send your mother to me. She and I have much to talk about."

Telemachus nodded and then left the hall, and Odysseus was alone. He gazed around the huge room, at the overturned furniture and the heaping platters of wasted, rotting food. The flickering torchlight illuminated the empty shelves. Where priceless treasures had once been proudly displayed, Odysseus now saw only dust.

"Stranger," Penelope said as she entered the dim banquet hall. "Please make yourself comfortable." She pointed toward a thick fleece rug near one of the huge fireplaces. Odysseus trotted over to it and lay down. Penelope sat in a polished highback wood chair beside him. "You find us in difficult times, and I'm afraid our hospitality is not what it should be."

"You owe me no explanations or apologies," Odysseus told her. "I have been treated kindly by you and your son. That is more than I could ever have hoped for."

"My son tells me that you are not like the other beggars we have met," Penelope told him. "I see he is right in what he says."

Smart lad, Odysseus thought. *Helping me with my disguise in case my language or behavior betrays my royal pedigree.* "I have lived differently from the way you see me now." *Is that ever true!*

101

"Please, tell me about yourself," Penelope said. "I am interested in far-off kingdoms—anywhere that is different from here."

Odysseus could see the sadness in his wife's lovely face. How he longed to bring her suffering to an end. It took all his strength not to blurt out that he was her long-absent husband. Then he realized Penelope was looking at him curiously. *I need to respond. I can't just lie here staring up at her.*

"I come from the far-off island of Crete," he said. "And I have had my share of troubles, which is why I appear to you as I do." He indicated his beggar's rags and his matted fur.

Penelope smiled sympathetically. "We have all known changes in fortune."

"It is kind of you to care for me when you have so much to worry about yourself," Odysseus said. "Your son has told me a little of your troubled situation."

Penelope sighed, shut her eyes, and leaned back in the chair. "My son has given away no secrets. Everyone in Ithaca knows that my happiness sailed away along with Odysseus, my dear husband. If only he would return home, together we could pick up the pieces of our lives and restore the palace and the kingdom to their former glory."

If only I could show you who I really am, Odysseus thought. *But for your own protection, I must keep my true identity hidden from you. Maybe I can comfort you by hinting that your husband is near and that he will be home soon.*

"I believe that I knew your husband, my lady," Odysseus said.

"Yes, my son mentioned that," Penelope told him. "But I have heard so many stories like that so many times, so I no longer know what to believe."

"You are wise to be careful, my lady. I ask for nothing but a warm night by this comforting fire, and your company for as long as you choose to give it," Odysseus said.

Penelope gazed at him for a moment. "You don't act anything like a beggar," she told him. "There is something so familiar about you. Although I cannot explain it, for some reason I feel I can trust you."

Odysseus knew the reason. *We were always so close that now, somehow, even disguised as this beggar, you can recognize me, my dear one.*

"I'm amazed that you have managed to go against the traditions and hold off the suitors," Odysseus said. "It can't have been easy."

"I did what I must." Penelope stood and paced the hall. "What upsets me now is that I'm having trouble thinking of new excuses to avoid a marriage."

"How were you able to prevent choosing a husband until now?" Odysseus asked. Knowing his wife, Odysseus figured her methods were tricky and clever.

"I set up a great loom in the hall and told the suitors I would marry one of them once I finished weaving a cloak," she explained. "They believed me and even stopped pestering me, fearful of wasting my time at the loom. Every day I sat there bent over the yarns. Then, every night, I would sneak down and unravel all the work I had done."

Odysseus's tail wagged in admiration. "That was a brilliant plan," he complimented the queen. *I don't think I could have done better myself.*

"Well, it worked only for a while," she admitted. "After three years, the suitors managed to guess something was not right. I was forced to finish the cloak. Now, once again, they insist that I choose a husband to be the new king."

She sighed and sat back down.

"I don't know what to do," she declared. "The longer they are here, the more of my son's inheritance they eat and drink. The kingdom has been turned topsy-turvy without a ruler. So many advise me just to accept that Odysseus is dead and gone."

Odysseus's heart nearly broke thinking about all the difficulties that Penelope had experienced during his long absence. *We are so alike,* he realized. *Each of us suffered our own hardships and trials, in our shared efforts to be reunited.*

"So tell me, stranger," Penelope said, "how did you come to meet my husband?"

Clearly she wants to change the subject. Odysseus wondered if she worried that she had said too much to a stranger. Once again, he felt a great desire to let her know who he was.

"Odysseus had been blown off course. He had his men anchor their vessel in a harbor near where I was living. He came into town, hoping someone could help him get directions," Odysseus told her. "Then a storm whipped up, delaying his departure. I offered him lodgings until the foul weather blew over. We passed several nights exchanging stories of our adventures, but his most touching words were of you."

Odysseus could see Penelope struggling to control the tears that threatened to stream down her face.

"Your husband's great love for you is as strong now as it was when he left the palace all those years ago—that I can promise you," Odysseus told Penelope. "It was all he could speak of, and he called you his 'bright and shining queen.'"

She took in a sharp breath at the familiar words. This time she couldn't fight her emotions any longer. Tears flowed down her face, and she wept for the memory of her lost husband.

"Ah, my queen," Odysseus said tenderly. "Ruin your lovely face no more with tears. I have news for you to gladden your heart."

Penelope gazed at him, her eyes glistening in the flickering torchlight. "Yes? What else have you to tell me?"

"I have heard that Odysseus is alive and makes

his way here. I am sure that as the old moon dies and the new moon rises into life, your Odysseus will return!"

"I wish with all my heart that your words will come true," Penelope said with emotion. Then deep sadness clouded her features, and she gazed down at the floor and shook her head. "No. I know too well what will happen. Time has run out and I must choose another king. Odysseus is gone."

"But my lady—" Odysseus protested immediately, but the sorrowful Penelope cut him off with firm shake of her head.

"I have been torn apart by hope before, and I cannot allow it to happen again," she told him. "The last of my conditions has been met. I promised the suitors that once a beard appeared on my son's face— once he became a man—I would remarry. And as you can see, my son is all grown up. I can think of no other way to delay my fate further."

That last condition is a tough one to get around, Odysseus thought. *Can't argue with whiskers.*

She prepared to leave the hall, but she paused in the doorway and glanced back at Odysseus. "Just knowing that you had been kind to my husband when he was lost makes you a dear friend. Is there anything you need that will make you more comfortable before I go to sleep?"

"Nothing, my lady," Odysseus replied. "You have already been more generous than you know."

"It has been good to talk with you," Penelope told Odysseus. "You know, you've just given me new hope. If what you say is really true, and Odysseus is still alive, then I must still find a way to continue to hold off the suitors."

"That's true!" He was relieved that she believed his news that her husband would return. Odysseus's tail wagged. "Do you have a plan, my lady?" he asked her eagerly, amazed that Penelope could be so clever despite her sorrow.

"Let me think." Penelope walked back to the chair and sat down beside Odysseus. She shut her eyes for a moment. Then a slow smile spread across her face. "Yes, I believe I do."

"Can you tell me?" Odysseus asked, regarding her with admiration. He loved her even more for her ability to keep rising above the ever-mounting obstacles.

"Odysseus had a very special bow. It was made of bronze, iron, and gold," she explained. "I will announce a challenge to the suitors. The man who can shoot an arrow clean through twelve standing battle axes using Odysseus's bow will be my next husband." Her smile broadened. "I have never seen anyone able to perform this exercise but Odysseus himself."

"Excellent idea, my lady!" His tail thumped with excitement.

"And now, I must bid you good night," the queen said. Odysseus held out his paw to shake. Then she stood. "I will see you tomorrow. And thank you. I have hope once again."

Well, my *hope is that the test is hard enough to keep* all *of the suitors from winning her hand,* Odysseus thought as he watched her leave the hall.

Odysseus tried to go to sleep, but he was too keyed up. He tossed and turned. Finally, he got up and headed downstairs for the kitchen, his toenails clicking on the hard wood floor. Before he reached the stairs, he passed a door that had been left slightly open. He overheard the sweet voice of his wife, Penelope. He ducked behind a chair to listen.

"Oh, Artemis, goddess, daughter of Zeus," said Penelope. "Pierce my heart with an arrow rather than allow me to marry a man I do not love."

Odysseus couldn't listen to his grief-stricken queen a moment longer. He couldn't stand to hear her plead for her own death. The misery caused by the suitors had gone on long enough.

Tomorrow I will succeed in righting the wrongs that have been committed in my absence. I must put an end to the suitors. Stop them I will!

CHAPTER ELEVEN

"Stop! I said stop, already!" Wishbone barked furiously. He poked his nose over the edge of the jaws of the bulldozer.

Whoa! The ground is a loooooong way down. No wonder no one can hear me. What a racket! The noise this bulldozer is making is deafening. It's even louder than Joe's favorite music.

"What does a dog say at a time like this?" Wishbone wondered. "Oh, I know. *Heelllpp!!!*"

He noticed David lower the video camera. "Wishbone?" David said.

David sees me! Wishbone got as close to the edge of the scoop as he dared. Then he barked even louder.

"*Yesss!* It's me! I'm on an express ride up, and I want to get off! Press the Down button, pull a lever—whatever it takes, please!"

Joe dashed out from between some trees and raced toward David. "David," he called. "I told Mom and Miss Gilmore—"

"Look!" David cut him off and pointed up at the bulldozer's mean-looking, jagged-toothed scoop.

Joe's eyes traveled up to where David was pointing. His mouth dropped open. "Wishbone?" Joe said. "Hey! Stop! Hey! My dog's up there! Hey!"

"What?" the driver in the bulldozer shouted over the noise of the earth-moving machine.

Wishbone watched Joe run over to the side of the cab. "Hurry!" Wishbone urged his friend.

"My dog!" Joe shouted. "He's up in there!"

The driver peered through the windshield. "How did . . . ?" He shook his head. "Forget it. Hang on. I'll bring him down."

Wishbone felt the bulldozer jerk, knocking him off his four feet. "I'm not afraid. I'm not afraid," he chanted over and over to himself, as he scrambled to stand back up.

Slowly the jaws lowered Wishbone to the ground.

"I'm not afraid. I'm not afraid." Wishbone felt the jaws hit the ground and he leaped out of his temporary prison. He dashed away from the bulldozer as fast as his four legs would take him. "I *was* afraid! I was *very* afraid!"

He lowered his nose to the dirt and took in its comforting earthy smell.

"Yes! *Terra firma!* It's good to be back on solid ground again." Then he ran over to Joe, who knelt down beside him and patted him all over.

"You okay, boy?"

Wishbone's tail wagged as he licked Joe's nose. "Thanks, Joe," he said. "Not that I was scared or anything. I've been in tougher spots than that. Did I ever tell you about the time—"

"I got it all on videotape," David interrupted, patting his video camera.

"Great!" Joe congratulated him. "And we got the construction crew to stop digging for now, at least."

Wishbone went over to the bulldozer and lay a paw on its tire. "You hear that? No more digging in my favorite spot!"

"I hope you're right," David said. "But we need somebody official to stop them. Otherwise, they'll destroy the area before we have a chance to get to the town council meeting."

Wishbone raced back over to the boys. "We can't let that happen!" *Hmm . . . just in case, maybe I'd better start getting my best stuff.* He scanned the area. *I think I buried a ball by that bush. And that other sock—it's got to be around here somewhere.*

"Hey! What's going on here?" Mr. King stalked out of the bushes. Wishbone noticed the man didn't look very happy. "I thought that this tree was coming down."

"Well, you thought wrong, buddy," Wishbone told Mr. King. Then he went over to Joe and stood by him. "So there!"

"This is not a playground," Mr. King declared. "You kids have to stay clear the construction site, or somebody's going to get hurt."

"It's not going to be a construction site for long if we have anything to say about it," Joe said.

"You tell him, Joe!" Wishbone let loose with a few encouraging barks.

"Excuussse me!"

Wishbone whirled around at the sound of Wanda Gilmore's singsong voice. She was followed by a slim man in a suit, carrying a briefcase. Then Wishbone glanced back up at Mr. King and said, "Well, it looks as if our reinforcements have arrived."

"Excuussse me!" Wanda repeated, as she made her way over to Mr. King. "Are you Mr. King of Suitor Development Corporation?"

"Yes, ma'am," Mr. King replied. Wishbone could see the businessman eyeing Wanda suspiciously.

You're right to be worried, Wishbone thought. *Wanda has a thing about digging up plants. Believe me, you don't want to be on the wrong side of a pile of dirt if Wanda is around.*

Wanda stood directly in front of Mr. King and planted her hands firmly on her hips. "I'm Wanda Gilmore of the Oakdale Arbor Society, and I don't like the way you do business."

Wishbone thought Mr. King suddenly looked a lot less friendly.

"What do you mean, lady?" he asked Wanda.

"You're sneaky," she told him. "You came in here so fast that you thought the neighborhood wouldn't know what hit it. Well, thanks to these kids, we're on to you, mister."

Wishbone glanced back at Joe and David. "Good job, guys." They smiled proudly, and David held up the video camera.

Mr. King shook his head. He looked directly into Wanda's accusing eyes. "Lady, I don't care what you think about me or how I conduct my business. The fact remains that I have every legal right to build a shopping center on this property."

"Come on, Wanda," Wishbone urged. "Don't let this guy threaten you."

Wishbone was pleased to see that Wanda didn't back off. Instead, she took a step closer to Mr. King. *Way to go, Wanda!* Wishbone thought. *Now it's your turn to threaten* him!

"Not so fast, buster," Wanda declared. "By this time tomorrow, our petition to stop you will be on the agenda for the town council meeting. We'll put a stop to this shameful destruction of nature. In the meantime, here's a restraining order that will keep you off this property."

Wishbone sat back on his haunches, waving his right front paw. "Woo! Go, Wanda, go!"

Wanda reached out her hand. The man in the suit standing behind her gave her an envelope. She smiled and presented the envelope to Mr. King.

Mr. King tore it open and scanned the paper inside. "W-what?" Mr. King sputtered. He glared at Wanda. "Lady, this building project of mine represents

113

important economic development for this entire area. You're not going to be able to stop it."

"And you won't get away with this without a fight!" Wanda shot back.

You tell 'im, Wanda! Wishbone jumped up and spun in the air. Then he dashed in front of Mr. King and barked at him. "If it's a fight you want, it's a fight you'll get!"

Mr. King turned abruptly and then stomped off into the distance.

The group stood silently as they watched the businessman leave the area.

"Okay, gang," Wishbone said. "We just bought ourselves a little bit of time, but we still have a way to go. So what next?"

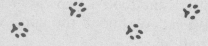

Just because Wanda was able to get a restraining order, it doesn't mean our work is done—far from it!

Odysseus also finds himself in his toughest battle of all only after he has already hit the home stretch.

CHAPTER TWELVE

Odysseus awoke to the irritating sounds of the suitors returning to the banquet hall. He got up onto his paws, yawned, and stretched his four legs. He watched the bullies tripping over one another, trying to be the first to give a lavish present to Penelope.

We requested your presents, Odysseus thought, *not your* presence. *So why don't you guys just drop off your gifts and then scram?*

"Where is she?" Antinous demanded. "We have brought treasures for the queen."

One of Penelope's ladies-in-waiting came into the banquet hall. "My lady has instructed me to tell you to bring your gifts into the courtyard," she announced.

Grumbling, the suitors carried their presents out into the entrance courtyard. *It's a good thing they did, too,* Odysseus thought. *Wouldn't want to break any of those trinkets during the battle that is to come.*

Eumaeus entered, watching the activities with worry. Odysseus saw the old swineherd's eyes scan the room, seeking him out. When he spotted Odysseus, Eumaeus hurried over to him. "Are you all right?" the swineherd asked Odysseus. "Was there any trouble here after I left?"

Odysseus shook his head, grateful for the man's concern. "Everything is under control," he told the kind swineherd. "Thank you for worrying about me, but have no fear—I can take care of myself," he replied. *And soon I shall take care of the suitors,* he added silently.

The suitors tumbled back into the banquet hall, demanding to be fed. "Let's talk about our plans to kill Telemachus later," Odysseus overheard Eurymachus whisper to Antinous. "Let's concentrate on feasting right now, instead."

Telemachus strode into the hall and walked up to Odysseus. "Beggar," he declared loudly enough for all the suitors to hear, "you sit and enjoy your meal. I will defend you against anyone who might try to harm you. All those here are ordered to treat you with respect."

"Big words," Antinous said sarcastically. "But don't worry, I'm too hungry to bother with the likes of a lowly beggar."

"If you are giving orders, Telemachus," one of the suitors shouted, "why don't you order your mother to marry one of us?"

"It is not my son's decision to make, but mine!" Penelope's strong voice carried through the hall. She stepped into the room in a regal manner.

Odysseus sat back on his haunches, surprised by his wife's appearance. Her eyes flashed with fire and she stood proud and strong, every inch a queen. In her arms she held his hunting bow. Slung over her shoulder was his case of bristling arrows. Behind her, Odysseus noticed her ladies-in-waiting, their arms loaded with twelve heavy bronze-and-iron battle axes.

"I have come to a decision," she said. "You claim you are all here only because you wish to marry me. Fine. I want to put an end to your siege of my palace once and for all. If the only way to do that is for me to marry one of you, then I shall. But I want to choose well and wisely. Therefore, in order to decide who I should marry, I present a great challenge."

She strode across the room and set the bow down on the long table. She took the case of arrows from her shoulder and laid it beside the weapon.

"Well, here it is. The man who can shoot one of these arrows clean through the lineup of all these axes is the man whom I shall marry—him and no other."

And that man will be none other than yours truly, Odysseus thought.

Then Penelope turned to Eumaeus, who stood by Odysseus. "Eumaeus, please set up these axes for the competition."

"This is just another trick," Antinous accused Penelope. "The test is too hard—no one can possibly do what you demand."

She smiled at the suitor. "Odysseus could do it," she replied calmly.

And I will again, Odysseus promised silently. *Thanks to that merit badge I earned in archery.*

"Are you happy now, men?" Telemachus said. "You have my mother's word that whoever meets her challenge shall be her husband." He let his eyes travel around the room. "That is, if there is one among you who is man enough. So, why the delay, fellows? Let the contest begin!"

By the time Telemachus finished speaking and sat down, Eumaeus had plunged the axes into the wood floor in a long, straight line. They stood as stiff as soldiers, their blades gleaming, with the small openings between the blade and the handle lined up perfectly.

Telemachus got up and strode to the table and lifted his father's heavy bow. "Well? You all boast and brag about your many skills. Here is your chance to prove you aren't just all talk." He laid the bow back down on the table and turned to his mother. "I guess no one here is up to the challenge. I suppose you shall remain without a husband a little longer, Mother." He returned to his seat.

"I'll try!" someone shouted.

"Me, too!"

"We *all* will!"

Odysseus lay back down, resting his nose on his paws. *I have a feeling we're going to be here all day.*

Antinous stepped up to the table, picked up an arrow, and lifted the bow, feeling its weight. "No problem," he bragged. "Everyone else may as well go home now, since I will win this contest."

In your dreams, Antinous, Odysseus thought, as he watched the suitor hold up the bow and take aim.

Antinous shut one eye, measuring the distance to the target. Then he pulled back on the bow. Odysseus could see Antinous's arm muscle straining from the tension in the string of the bow.

Come on, already! Odysseus urged. *Shoot!*

Thwack! Antinous released the arrow and it zipped from the bow—straight into the first axe. It clattered as it landed on the floor.

"Gee, tough luck, Antinous," Odysseus said as the suitors laughed. "What's the matter—did the sun get in your eyes?"

"Quiet!" Antinous snarled, hurling the bow to the floor. "I'd like to see any of you do better."

Eurymachus dashed over to the bow and lifted it into place. "I'll do it!" he declared. He readied an arrow, then took aim, standing very still.

Odysseus shook his head. *What are you waiting for—your beard to grow?*

Eurymachus sent the arrow sailing—right over the axes. He, too, flung down the bow in anger.

Each suitor tried and failed. Odysseus stood up and trotted over to the bow. *Let's get this over with, once and for all.*

"I wonder if my twisted old limbs still have their former power," he said.

Just to annoy them, I think I'll really play up the old-and-frail-beggar act. Besides, it will keep them off guard if they believe they have nothing to fear from me.

"How about if I give it a try?" He lifted the bow.

Several of the suitors began to laugh and jeer.

"No!" Antinous shouted. "This is an outrage!"

"Are you crazy?" Eurymachus exclaimed. "Do you think we would let a lowly beggar accept Penelope's challenge? It is an insult to us all."

"Silence!" Penelope commanded. "If he wants to try his hand, we should let him. Are you afraid he will succeed where you have failed?"

119

"And what if he wins?" Eurymachus demanded. "Will you marry him?"

"I will follow the rules I have set before you," Penelope replied. "I expect the same from all of you."

Odysseus had to duck his head to hide his smile. *Don't mess with her, boys. She means business.* Then he realized this would be a good time to have Telemachus take the queen to a safe place without causing suspicion. Odysseus knew there would be trouble after his attempt with the bow. He caught his son's eye and jerked his head in Penelope's direction. Telemachus nodded, indicating that he understood.

"Mother," Telemachus said, "I think your being here distracts the men. Why don't you and your ladies return to your rooms, while I run the contest? And have no fear," he promised before she could protest. "I will allow the beggar to take up the bow."

"Perhaps you are right, son," Penelope replied. "I don't think that I have the heart to watch this event go to its end."

After all of the women had cleared the hall, Odysseus raised the bow. The suitors shouted their objections all around him, but he ignored their cries. He loved the familiar feeling of the beautiful bow in his paws. He placed an arrow carefully, taking aim. Still the suitors laughed and yelled, trying to distract him.

He gripped the arrow in his teeth, pulling it back, back, back. . . . Then—*zip!*—he released the arrow. It flew through the air, straight and true. It sailed smoothly through the hole in each of the twelve axes, then plunged into the tapestry that hung from the wall behind the axes.

"Not bad for an old beggar," Odysseus said, as he placed the bow carefully back down on the table. The suitors gaped at him, too stunned to move or speak.

"H-h-how were you able to do that?" Antinous finally stammered.

"Practice," Odysseus replied. "Oh, yeah, and talent." Then he leaped up onto the table. "Okay, game over! My mother always taught me to clean up when I was done playing. And this place could definitely use some cleaning up!"

Odysseus braced himself for the change, his paws planted firmly on the table so that he would stay steady. The strength returned to his four legs. Next, he felt the dirt lift from his fur. The suitors stared in amazement as Odysseus changed from the old, hunched beggar in rags back into the heroic king. *Thank you, Athena,* he thought, knowing she must be somewhere nearby.

Several men dropped to their knees in terror. "Who are you?" someone shouted.

Okay, it's show time. "It is I, King Odysseus. I have returned." He gazed out at the crowd. "And you guys are in for some major trouble! You're all about ready to be exiled to the doghouse!"

CHAPTER THIRTEEN

"Hey!" Joe cried, pointing at the television screen. "It's Wishbone!" It was after dinner. Joe, Sam, David, and Emily were sitting in the Talbots' living room and watching the video that David had shot in the woods earlier in the day.

"Where? How do I look?" Wishbone peered at the screen. There he was, barking furiously from the cold steel jaws of the bulldozer's scoop. "How brave! How handsome! And I do all my own stunts, you know."

"Wishbone, you're blocking our view," David complained.

"Sit over here, Wishbone," Emily said, patting the spot beside her on the couch.

"Uh . . . no, thanks, Emily. I'm fine right here." Wishbone edged closer to the TV and sat down. "You look sweet and cute, but looks can be deceiving. If I let my guard down even for a moment—*wham!*—back to solitary confinement."

"Uh-oh," Emily said. "There's the man making all the trouble."

Wishbone raised himself up and whirled around, planting his four feet to be ready for action. "Where? Just let me at him!" Then he noticed where Emily was looking. "Oh, you mean Mr. King on the video. *Phew!*" He sat back down. *That was a close call. But did I back down from danger? No way!*

"Well, that's it," David said, clicking off the tape. "That's everything I got."

"Shooting the video was a great idea," Sam told David. "I think it showed Mr. King that we really mean business."

"And it's also evidence that Mr. King is rushing ahead with the construction before he's supposed to," Ellen added as she came into the living room. She sat on the arm of the couch.

A car horn honked, and Wishbone darted to the window. "It's your dad, Sam," Wishbone told her.

"I think that's my dad," Sam said. "I have to go." She grabbed her backpack from a corner of the room.

"We'd better go also, Emily," David said.

Ellen, Joe, and Wishbone walked them to the front door. "'Bye!" Wishbone called, as Sam headed toward her car, and David and Emily went next door to their house. "I'll see you guys tomorrow at the town council meeting."

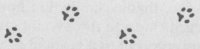

"Nope, sorry, never heard that 'no pets allowed' rule." Wishbone crawled under Joe's seat and tried as

best he could to make himself invisible. *That's my story, and I'm sticking to it.*

Ellen stood at a podium in the room where the town council met. She held some note cards. "The word *ecology* comes from the Greek word *öko,* which means 'household,'" she said into the microphone. "Our community thinks of this unique tree and the land around it as part of our town's household. It's a backyard that everyone shares. Therefore, it only makes sense that this property be attached to Jackson Park for all to enjoy. Thank you."

She picked up her note cards and then returned to her seat.

"Well done, Ellen," Wishbone said. "You didn't happen to bring any doggie treats in your purse, did you? This meeting has gone on a whole lot longer than I expected it would."

Wanda approached the podium and smiled over at Ellen. "Thank you, Ellen." Then she turned to face the council members, who sat at a long conference table. "I'm sure all of you remember Ellen from your visits to the Henderson Memorial Library, where she is the reference librarian. Her testimony, along with what you've heard from all my friends at the Oakdale Arbor Society, must certainly convince each and every one of you of the urgency of the matter at hand. We need to stop the Suitor Development Corporation before it's too late."

Wishbone peered out from under Joe's chair, looking for Mr. King. *There he is. That's right, start sweating, buddy, because you're not going to be King of the hill much longer!*

"In the event that you aren't all completely convinced," Wanda continued, "I offer the testimony of three people who are growing up in this community. What kind of Oakdale will we hand over to them? Shall we allow the likes of Mr. King to determine the quality of their future?"

Mr. King squirmed again.

"Don't let the mild expressions on the faces of those Oakdale Arbor Society ladies fool you," Wishbone warned. "Those women mean business."

Wanda glanced around at the assembled townspeople. Next, she called her first witness. "David?" she said, then moved away from the mike.

"Ooh! She's bringing in her heavy hitters now," Wishbone said.

David stepped up to the mike, lowered it slightly, and cleared his throat. "Ladies and gentlemen of the council, my name is David Barnes. I'm twelve years old and I've lived here all my life. At first, I thought it was a pretty good idea to have a Tastee Oasis so close to where I live. I could have gone there just about any time I wanted to."

He grinned sheepishly at the crowd in the room. Several people chuckled, and Ellen gave him an encouraging smile.

"But then, I probably would have gotten sick of it after a while," David went on. "The thing is, I know I'll never get sick of the bike path or the trees on my way to the park. They've been there a long time, and I don't think anybody's ever gotten tired of looking at them. Does the world really need another Tastee Oasis? I don't think so. Thank you."

David stepped aside to allow Joe to take his place at the microphone.

Now, don't be nervous, Joe, Wishbone urged. *Lots of eye contact and a clear, strong voice are always your best weapons.*

Joe gazed at the audience before he looked at his notes and began to speak. "My name's Joe Talbot," he told them. "I just want to say that I think it would be awful to cut down all those trees, especially that big old oak. When I was a little kid, I used to go to that one with my dad. There's a tire swing there, and he used to swing me on it. After my dad died, my mom and I would go there. It was a good place to hang out and think about him. I know that tree belongs to everybody, but a part of it belongs to me and my dad."

Perfect, Joe—not a single slipup. Wishbone felt proud of his friend. *I taught you everything I know about public speaking.*

Joe returned to his seat, next to Ellen. He reached

down to stick his notes back inside his backpack. Wishbone gave his pal's hand a congratulatory lick. Joe peered under the chair, and his eyes widened when he discovered Wishbone.

"Don't let anyone know I'm here," Wishbone cautioned. "They've got some silly rule about no pets inside." Wishbone pulled his head farther under the chair. "Check it out, Joe. Sam's up."

Joe gave Wishbone a pat, then sat back up. Wishbone's tail thumped as he watched Sam approach the podium. *Good plan, having Sam in the cleanup position. We'll hit a home run for sure!*

"I'm Samantha Kepler," she said. "Everybody in our neighborhood can tell a story about the big tree. But the tree itself also has a story to tell us. It tells us the story of summer when it's hot and we sit under its shade. It tells us the story of fall, when its leaves turn red and yellow, and cover the ground. Winter is a story of branches when they're bare. And then comes the part about spring, when the green comes back again. Every time one story ends, another begins. That's what the big old oak tree tells us. If we destroy it, we lose the story forever. Please let us keep it."

The room was silent as Samantha left the podium and returned to her seat. Wishbone whipped his head back and forth so fast his ears flapped. *Why is everybody so quiet?* he wondered.

Then Wanda Gilmore suddenly leaped to her feet and began to applaud. Soon the whole room was standing and clapping.

The council members looked at one another and nodded. They seemed to have reached a decision. "The council has determined that the land in question shall become a part of Jackson Park," the mayor announced, pounding his gavel on the table.

The room went wild.

Wishbone jumped out from under the chair and did a flip. He noticed that Mr. King didn't look too happy.

"You didn't think we had it in us, did you?" Wishbone asked the businessman. "Well, it's amazing what a group of friends can accomplish when they put their heads and their hearts together!"

CHAPTER FOURTEEN

A great roar went up in the banquet hall as the suitors watched Odysseus change from beggar to warrior-hero. Then they realized that their missing king had in fact returned to his rightful place. They cringed as they realized that the man who ruled them all had witnessed their terrible behavior. Terror moved the suitors into immediate action. They raced for the exit doors, the windows—any way to escape the severe punishment they knew awaited them.

"Where are you going?" Odysseus called. "Is the party over?" He slung the case of arrows across his back and grabbed the bow. "And I thought the fun was just starting." He leaped from the table.

Antinous raced toward Odysseus, gripping a small dagger aimed to slice the king's throat.

"Have a nice trip. See you next fall," Odysseus taunted. He tugged a small rug covering the floor with his teeth and sent Antinous sprawling.

Eurymachus lunged for Telemachus, but the

young prince hurled a handful of mashed potatoes at him. They landed in his attacker's face, blinding him long enough for Telemachus to grab the man's sword and toss it aside.

"Telemachus, one! The suitors, zero!" Odysseus cheered.

Telemachus hurled fruits and vegetables at the mob, and the suitors grabbed small tables and stools to try to shield themselves. Then they banged into one another in their desperate attempt to flee.

Odysseus spotted a suitor sneaking up behind Telemachus. "Look behind you!" he shouted.

Telemachus glanced over his shoulder and then banged the suitor on the head with his bronze shield. "Thanks, Dad!" Telemachus gave Odysseus a thumbs-up sign.

"Great teamwork!" Odysseus shouted.

With a scream of fury, Eurymachus scrambled off the floor. He grabbed a lighted torch from the wall and came after Odysseus.

"Sorry," Odysseus quipped. "I didn't bring any marshmallows, and this isn't the time for a weenie roast." He let fly an arrow, pinning Eurymachus to the wall by his tunic. His feet dangled a few inches above the ground. Then he nipped at the heels of the last of the suitors as he chased them out.

Soon father and son looked all around the nearly empty banquet hall.

"Now, those were really *some* odds," Odysseus commented. "Two against many. They never had a chance."

Penelope burst into the banquet hall. She

clutched her son, pulling him close to her in a tight embrace. "I heard all the noise, and I was afraid the suitors had done their worst." She glanced around. "But . . . but where are they?"

"They're gone, Mother," Telemachus assured her. "For good. Their siege is over. And now, a sight that will fill you with joy," Telemachus told his mother. He nodded toward Odysseus.

Penelope's brow furrowed in confusion as she glanced back and forth between Telemachus and Odysseus.

"Mother, don't you recognize him?" Telemachus cried. "It is your husband, my father, Odysseus. He has returned, and together we fought off the suitors."

"I-I-I am filled with complete wonder," Penelope stammered. "Can it be true?"

Odysseus wagged his tail and raised a paw for her to take. "Yes, my dear queen. The goddess Athena disguised me as the beggar you so kindly brought into your home."

Penelope gazed at him, amazement in her eyes, but Odysseus could also see doubt.

"Are you still unsure, my love?" he asked, his round brown eyes searching her face.

"You look much as he did when he left here so many years ago," she admitted. "But how do I know for sure that you are truly my missing husband? Gods sometimes play cruel tricks by appearing in the form of loved ones." She shook her head, as if to clear it. "You will live here with us until we determine if you are truly Odysseus or not."

"Mother!" Telemachus said in shock.

133

"No, your mother is right to be careful," Odysseus said. "Looks can be tricky. I am not offended. You know, it's not every day that a wife discovers her long-lost husband is back, and is also a quick-change artist. It takes a little getting used to."

"Thank you for understanding my confusion," Penelope told Odysseus. "I just need some time to make sure that you are who you claim to be."

Then the queen turned to her son.

"Telemachus, you must move the bed your father built from my chamber for the stranger here to sleep in," Penelope instructed. "Odysseus made it with his own hands. I know this fellow will find it comfortable."

"No man on this earth could move that bed!" Odysseus exclaimed. "How can Telemachus lift a bed made from the carved-out hollow of an enormous olive tree?" He gazed at Penelope. "Unless you took an axe to it and chopped it down."

At those words, Penelope dropped to her knees and flung her arms around Odysseus's neck. "It *is* you!" she cried. "At long last, you have returned!" Tears streamed freely down her face. They were tears of joy, not sorrow. "That was the final test, my love. No one but the builder himself knows the story of the tree-bed."

"We are a family again!" Telemachus declared.

Penelope opened her arms to include their son in their embrace. Finally, Odysseus sat back on his haunches and gazed at his wife and son, his tail wagging in joy. "This is the moment I imagined throughout my journey. Knowing that some day we would be together again gave me the will and strength to battle every obstacle along the way."

Loud shouts made Odysseus's fur bristle.

"What's that?" the king wondered, dashing over to the large windows, with Penelope and Telemachus right behind him.

"People have surrounded the palace!" Penelope gasped.

It was true. A huge crowd spread across the front courtyard, yelling taunts at the palace. The escaped suitors had returned, and with them they had brought reinforcements.

"What do we do?" Telemachus asked.

Odysseus didn't need to answer. There, high above the crowd, the goddess Athena hovered. "There is to be no more fighting!" she commanded in her strong, pure voice. "It ends here."

A gasp went through the mob. Some screamed; others fainted dead away at the sight of the shining goddess. *Good ol' Athena,* Odysseus thought. *She always did enjoy making a grand entrance and speaking to a captive audience.*

"Odysseus defended his home and family from the suitors, as he should. He fought the traitors and won," Athena continued. "He is not to be punished for this. Those men got what they deserved."

A lightning bolt split the sky and someone cried out, "Zeus himself!" More of the crowd dropped to their knees. Others clutched each other in fear.

Athena smiled. "Yes, that is a sign from Zeus to seal the pact. You are to agree that Odysseus is once again king, and you all shall live together in peace." She turned to face Odysseus at the window. "That goes for you, too, Odysseus."

The king waved a paw at her. "Whatever you say, Athena."

"So it shall be," she commanded. "For now and always."

"So it shall be," King Odysseus repeated, taking Queen Penelope's hand in one paw, and Telemachus's hand in the other.

CHAPTER FIFTEEN

"We heroes have all returned!" Wishbone announced. He gazed around the woodlands proudly. It was the day after the town council meeting. Wishbone and all his friends had come to have a celebratory picnic under the big oak tree.

"That hard work was all worth it," Wanda said, strolling over to the big oak tree. "What a magnificent tree this is."

Emily dashed up to the tree and patted its bark. "Feel better, tree? You're safe. No one's going to cut you down now."

"I know *I* feel better," Wishbone said. He dug into the dirt with his paws and uncovered a sock. "Yes! It's still here. No permanent damage." He then quickly kicked the dirt back over it with his hind legs to rebury his treasure.

"You kids did great," Ellen told David, Sam, and Joe, as she set down the basket and blanket she was carrying. "I really think it was hearing from you three that made up the council's mind."

"Thanks, Mom. I'm really glad we did it," Joe said. "Even if I *was* nervous."

"We all were," Sam added.

Joe and David helped Ellen spread the picnic blanket under the oak tree's broad canopy of leaves. Sam and Wanda set up an easel a few feet away.

"I love picnics," Wishbone declared. "All of this delicious food right at ground level."

Joe sat down and began to strum a guitar. Ellen pulled a tattered old copy of *The Odyssey* out of her shoulder bag, flipped it open, and settled back against the tree. Wanda perched herself on a little stool at the easel and set up her paints. Sam and David tossed a ball back and forth, while Emily drew in a coloring book.

Everyone is doing one of his or her favorite activities, Wishbone observed. "And *mine* is eating!" Wishbone announced.

The dog dashed over to the picnic basket, lifting the lid with his nose, and poked around inside. He was so overwhelmed by all the great smells, he wasn't sure which tasty dish to choose!

Perfect! Wishbone dragged a large drumstick out of the basket. "Anyone for a drumstick, raise your right hand. . . . No? I guess this one's mine." *Mmm-mmm.* Wishbone chewed happily on the meaty bone.

"Hey, Wishbone!" a voice shouted behind him.

Wishbone was so startled he dropped the bone. "Whoa! Emily, don't sneak up on a fellow like that. You could give a guy a heart attack."

Emily knelt down. "Nice doggie, doggie," she said. Then she broke off a small piece from her sandwich and held it out to Wishbone.

Wishbone's whiskers twitched, but he eyed her suspiciously. "Oh, no, no, no," Wishbone said, shaking his head. "You can fool Wishbone only once. I take a little tiny bite—and then it's right back in the wagon prison for me."

"Come on, Wishbone," Emily encouraged him. "You know you like bologna."

Wishbone's ears perked up. "Bologna?" he repeated. "You drive a hard bargain." He thought over the situation. "I guess I can always eat and run." He moved toward her very slowly, belly to the ground. "Careful . . . careful. Just close enough to grab the sandwich, but not close enough to be captured."

Emily sat down and tore off another piece of the sandwich and held it out.

Wishbone snatched it with his teeth and gulped it down. "Mmm-mmm, that's good."

Emily broke off another small piece.

Wishbone cocked his head. "Hey, Emily, how

about the big piece? You know—the one in your left hand. Yes, that's right—the rest of the sandwich. Please?"

Emily held out the small piece toward Wishbone.

"Well, it's a start." Wishbone took it with ease. "Delicious!"

"My friend, Wishbone." Emily scratched him between the ears.

Wishbone lay his nose on her leg and let her pet him. "Okay, Emily, I forgive you for trying to kidnap me and keep me from getting home. We're pals again."

Wishbone finished his snack, then dashed over to the large oak tree. He placed a paw on its trunk.

Well, tree, you survived, he thought. *Just like Odysseus. Thanks to loyalty, bravery, clever thinking, and never giving up. Oh, yeah—and a little help from your friends.*

About Homer

We know very little about the Greek poet Homer, who wrote one of the world's greatest epics, *The Odyssey*. Scholars believe that he lived in the late ninth or early eighth century B.C.—nearly 2,700 years ago! Almost no written records survive from Homer's time. In fact, very few people were able to write, so it's possible that the author of this exciting story never wrote it down!

What *is* known about Homer comes to us from historians who lived at a somewhat later time—around 2,300 years ago. Most scholars agree that Homer came from Chios, a city in Asia Minor, although several ancient cities later claimed him as a citizen. He was probably a traveling poet, an entertainer at religious festivals, public celebrations, and other important events. (In *The Odyssey*, a blind poet recites the story of the Trojan War; this has led many scholars to believe that Homer was blind.) These "singers of tales" recited, chanted, or sang heroic stories, often accompanied by musicians. Homer amazed his audience by improvising parts of the poem on the spot, all the while sticking to the strict rules of poetic rhythm and meter.

Reciting Homer's *Odyssey* had to be hard work—the poem is 12,109 lines long! Luckily for centuries of readers, he remembered it all, and someone, perhaps not Homer himself, wrote it down for us to continue to enjoy.

About *The Odyssey*

The English word *odyssey* comes from the title of this ancient epic poem and means "a long wandering voyage"—which basically sums up the story! *The Odyssey* is part of what is known as oral tradition—stories and poems that were told out loud. The poem must have been a big hit, because people knew it throughout the Mediterranean.

Back in Homer's time, few people could read or write, and the poem that we read today is based on copies dating from hundreds of years after Homer's death. (Some scholars believe that Homer wrote down some of his poem as he was composing it; others argue that he never learned the alphabet.) Even though we don't have the actual manuscript of the original, we have these very old copies that are probably close to what Homer himself created. Copies of *The Odyssey* were in circulation all over the Greek world in the fifth and fourth centuries B.C.

This poem was so popular and important that ancient scholars took the trouble to translate it into many languages. The first printed version of *The Odyssey* was published in 1488. Earlier copies had to be written out by hand, first on leather or papyrus rolls, in later years on parchment.

Scholars regard *The Odyssey* as one of the earliest and finest books ever written. With danger, magical challenges, and vivid characters, this poem has something for everyone from any time—especially for a brave Jack Russell terrier with a nose for adventure!

About Carla Jablonski

Carla Jablonski is a writer and an actress living in New York City. When she attended Vassar College, she studied ancient Greek and Greek history and mythology. Her studies introduced her to Homer's *The Odyssey*, and she still loves the Greek classics today. In fact, in her most recent play—an adaptation of the Greek tragedy *The Bacchae*—she even played the role of one of the gods!

Carla has taught writing and has also edited many of the *Choose Your Own Adventure* series of books. She worked on the *Hardy Boys* digest series and wrote the novelization for the TV show *Calling All Creeps*, an R.L. Stine *Goosebumps Presents* book. Her plays have been performed in New York City and Edinburgh, Scotland.

Being an actress has given Carla the opportunity to travel. While performing in a show in Israel, she visited Greece and viewed many of the places she read about in school. When Carla isn't writing or performing, she loves to cook—almost as much as Wishbone loves to eat!

WHAT HAS FOUR LEGS, A HEALTHY COAT, AND A GREAT DEAL ON MEMBERSHIP?